Mahi-Mahi Matrimony

Book 2 in The Second Chances DO Happen Series -- Sweet with a Hint of Spice!

Pat Adeff

Apollo Burps Productions

This book is dedicated to my own Second Chance, my husband, Todd.

Babe, for all you do, and for who you are, I love you!

Contents

Newsletter

To get notified on new releases, please go to
www.patadeff.com and sign-up!

Chapter One

WEDDING BELLS

Julie stood in front of the full-length mirror and looked in awe and disbelief at the pretty girl in the wedding dress.

The girl looked picture perfect.

Her hair was expertly coiffed under the wedding tiara and veil.

The long, beaded dress fit perfectly. The dress' design made her look taller.

Her make-up looked like a Hollywood make-up artist had done it for her.

Close – it was done by a Broadway make-up artist; someone the groom knew.

Why wasn't the girl in the mirror smiling and what was that haunted look in her eyes?

Julie didn't know how long she stood there staring at her reflection.

Was it time yet?

Actually, time didn't matter. They couldn't start without her; after all, she was the bride.

And she had an announcement that wouldn't go over very well with the family and friends waiting in the church.

Finally, the minister knocked on her dressing room door.

"Julie?" He tentatively opened the door and entered the room.

"Come on in." Julie turned from the mirror and stepped toward the cleric.

"Are you ready?" His eyes were somber and searching.

"As ready as I'll ever be." Julie tried on a small smile, found it fit okay, and sort of left it pasted on her mouth. Too bad it didn't reach her eyes.

Father Hanrahan offered his arm to Julie, but she grabbed his hand instead. He placed his other hand over their clenched ones and gave a firm pat.

"Let's get this done."

She couldn't have agreed more.

As they entered the front of the church from the side vestibule, Julie could see the questioning looks starting on some of the congregation's faces.

She could hear the murmurs starting.

Why wasn't she walking up the aisle?

Where was her bouquet?

And where was the groom?

Julie realized that seeing all her family and friends actually made her feel calmer.

She released Father Hanrahan's hand and stepped towards the front center of the altar area, facing everyone else.

It was very quiet for a few moments while she looked around and gave a small smile to the people in attendance.

Julie saw her mother's eyes cloud over as she seemed to realize what was happening and watched as her eyes finally dropped to her hands in her lap.

Julie saw her fiancé's parents look at each other in bewilderment.

Finally finding her voice, Julie addressed everyone.

"Hi." She was pleased that her voice hadn't quavered.

"I want to thank you all for coming today. I know that this isn't quite what you expected to see, but I'm afraid there's been a change."

Okay. So far, so good. Keep going and maybe you'll get through this with your dignity intact.

"I'm not quite sure how to say this, but I guess that the simplest way is to be direct."

You could have heard a pin drop in the silence that filled the church.

And in that silence is when Julie lost her voice. Seeing the sweet faces of her friends and family as it was slowly dawning on them, she could see that they were starting to understand what was about to come.

The realization of the betrayal many of them would feel deflated any courage she had.

Suddenly she couldn't speak.

She opened her mouth a couple of times to start and just couldn't find the breath to speak or the words that she'd so carefully rehearsed in the dressing room.

Mercifully, Father Hanrahan could see the pain she was in and stepped forward to stand next to her.

Taking her hand in his, he nodded once and then addressed everyone else in the church.

"Ladies and Gentlemen. Family and Friends. I'm sorry to announce that there won't be a wedding today."

3

Julie heard Spencer's mom inhale sharply from the front pew at the same time Julie's father blurted out "What the ...?"

As the minister continued explaining how Spencer had gotten with him a few minutes earlier and had decided that he couldn't marry Julie.

Julie could feel herself going into emotional shock. Her hands were getting cold, she couldn't catch her breath, and the room was getting dim.

She felt like she was softly falling into a feather bed as the lights finally went out.

Julie became vaguely aware of a mixture of voices. The first one she was able to sort out was her dad's strident tone.

"What do you mean Spencer can't get married? Where is he? I want to talk to him. Right now!" Every syllable pounded into Julie's head like an angry wake-up alarm.

The next voice was easily her mom's.

"Is she okay? Why isn't she waking up? Oh, my poor baby."

Julie knew that her mom's carefully measured tone of sorrow wouldn't ever get to the point that she actually shed tears – that would ruin her make-up. And heaven forbid she look less than perfect.

Julie really didn't want to open her eyes. She knew that as long as she was "unconscious" she wouldn't have to answer any questions.

However, the undergarments that made her wedding dress fit so nicely were really uncomfortable and she wanted to change into her travel outfit as soon as possible.

She'd be danged if she was going to let the honeymoon arrangements, and expense, go to waste. In the few moments after Spencer had explained to her why he was unable to marry her, Julie's heart had hardened.

She became determined to finally put a stop to the charade of the life she'd been living for the past few years, trying to please her parents, Spencer, pretty much everyone, including her best friend, Charlotte.

Charlotte – who just happened to be the reason Spencer could no longer marry Julie.

Charlotte, who was no longer her best friend.

Sigh. *Come on, coward. Time to face the music.*

Julie opened her eyes.

When the room finally stopped spinning, Julie was able to focus first on her mom. She was sitting daintily on the edge of one of the settee's in the bride's room, a lace handkerchief in one perfectly manicured hand.

"Oh, Baby! You're awake! I'm so happy."

Julie smiled at her mom. She seemed actually happy to see Julie wake up.

"Hi, Mom."

Julie attempted to sit up. When she had to brace a hand to get her balance, her dad moved over to her and helped her sit up straight.

He sat on the edge of the settee next to her, keeping a steadying hand on Julie's shoulder.

"Hey, Sweetie. How are you doing?" Her dad had always had a way to shift instantly from anger to caring. It almost made her tear up.

Her mom's version of caring never seemed to reach Julie's heart, but her dad's caring always hit like a bullseye.

"Hey, Daddy." Julie was able to smile at him. "I'm okay."

"For goodness sake, Julie, what happened? What did you do?"

Leave it to Mom to get right to the point. If something bad happened, it had to be something that Julie did or had failed to do.

"Actually, Mom. This time it was something that Spencer did, as hard as that might be to understand."

Julie was pretty amazed that her voice sounded so calm.

Julie's dad had already turned towards his wife with a look of astonishment on his face.

There were times his wife just went beyond the pale, and this was one of them.

"Margo! Please."

Something silent passed between them and Julie could see her mom silently agree with her dad's plea.

"I'm sorry, Julie. I guess I'm a little bit overwhelmed at the moment. Please forgive me."

At this point, Julie realized that she wouldn't have to undergo the third degree from her mom. She felt herself relax a little.

"It's okay, Mom. It was a shock to me too."

"Can you tell us what happened?" Her dad truly looked perplexed.

"Well, as far as I can tell, Spencer fell in love with Charlotte and out of love with me."

It hadn't been as difficult to state as Julie thought it would have been. In fact, she was aware that she should have felt more emotion, but she didn't.

Julie could see that her mom wasn't understanding.

"What do you mean? Charlotte? Your Maid of Honor?"

"Yep, that's the one." Julie was able to stand up now and did so.

While her parents looked from her to each other in puzzlement, Julie stated, "I'm going to change out of this dress. By the way, Mom. It was beautiful. Thank you."

Julie grabbed the hanger with her travel outfit and slipped into the bathroom before anyone could ask another question.

When Julie finally stepped back out into the parlor area of the dressing room, it appeared that Father Hanrahan had been speaking with her parents and they'd come to a decision of some sort.

"Honey." Her dad started out. "I can get you a refund of your trip to Turks and Caicos if you want."

"Actually, Dad. I'm going on my now non-honeymoon. I think I've earned a vacation."

Julie's wry smile brought a small matching one to her dad's face. "I need some time to think and this will give me the perfect chance."

Julie almost laughed out loud when she realized that she was going to use her paid vacation time accrued from her job at Spencer's advertising firm.

She didn't think that Spencer was going to object. Even if he wanted to, he really couldn't. Not after the stunt he'd just pulled.

The little bit of anger that tinged her viewpoint right now felt invigorating.

"Mom. Dad. I'm asking that you trust me on this. We'll talk when I get back in a couple of weeks. Right now, this is what I need to do."

In response, Julie's dad picked up her suitcase and her mom walked her to the door in a silence of perplexed agreement.

When they got to the limo, Julie saw that someone had made sure all the "Just Married" signs and balloons had been removed from the vehicle.

She shot a smile of thanks to Father Hanrahan who just nodded back at her.

After hugging her mom and dad, Julie settled into the soft leather of the spacious back seat of the vehicle that was taking her to the airport.

She rolled down her window and waved goodbye to the small ensemble who had gathered on the driveway of the church to see her off; Father Hanrahan, her mom and dad, the church office secretary, and her Aunt Esther, her dad's slightly off-center older sister.

"Goodbye, Julie! Have a great honeymoon!"

Julie could only smile at her aunt's enthusiastically inappropriate salutation and the way her dad rolled his eyes.

The limo pulled away from the church and Julie rolled up her window and faced forward. There was a single champagne glass sitting in a holder waiting for her.

Without thinking about her lack of food that day, Julie downed the refreshment in just a few swallows. As the warmth hit her ears first, she sighed and relaxed into the seat.

The window that separated her from the driver rolled down. "If you want, there is a sandwich in the small cupboard to your right."

Julie thanked the driver and the window rolled back up. She just bet that he didn't want to have to deal with a hysterically drunk non-bride.

As she bit into the chicken and walnut-salad sandwich, Julie's appetite came back with a vengeance.

As she savored the bits of cranberry added to the mix, it only took her a few bites to demolish the food.

Finding a bottle of water in the same cupboard, Julie washed it down with satisfaction.

She was surprising herself a bit with her lack of upset.

She would have thought that getting stood up at the altar would be more emotional.

Maybe she was in shock and the loss would hit her later in spades.

Either way, she now had a couple of stress-free weeks to deal with the aftermath.

Of course, she would submit her resignation to the company. To Spencer's company.

When she'd first landed the job as photographer for the tony advertising firm in NYC, Julie felt like she'd been handed the prize.

When the owner and CEO, Spencer, started paying attention to her, she felt lucky to get his mentoring.

When their relationship grew into more, she struggled with what she considered the unprofessionalism of their relationship.

Even though Spencer didn't seem to have a problem with it, Julie felt that the rest of the employees had shifted slightly away from her, as though she was no longer one of the office gang.

When it became apparent that she and Spencer were getting serious, she found herself not getting invited any longer for after work drinks or get-togethers with the office workers.

The rolling down of the limo's separation window interrupted her musings.

"Do you need anything, Miss?" The driver looked like he wanted to be anywhere but in that particular limo, driving this particular almost-bride.

When Julie realized she was less concerned about her present predicament than the driver, she laughed out loud.

"Would you mind terribly pulling over?" She smiled at the driver when his brows furrowed.

"Are you okay?"

"I'm fine. But could we please pull over for a moment?"

"Of course, Miss."

As the limo slid to a stop on the side of the road, Julie reached for the door handle before the driver understood what she was going to do.

He immediately exited the driver's door when he saw Julie step out of the vehicle.

"Do you mind if I sit up front with you? I really don't want to be in the back."

If the driver was thrown off by her request, he recovered rapidly and scooted around to the passenger door for the front seat.

As she slid into the bucket seat in front, which actually was much more comfortable than the wide couch-like seat in the back, Julie felt much better.

When the driver got back into the car, Julie turned to him.

"What is your name?"

"It's Dave, Miss."

"And mine's Julie. Please drop the "Miss." It's sort of a reminder of my not-Mrs. status."

When Dave's eyes widened and he started to stammer out an apology, Julie burst into laughter.

"It's okay. I was only partially kidding you. But your response was great. I needed the laughter. Thank you!"

Dave smiled across at Julie and she grinned back.

"How long until we get to the airport?"

"About twenty minutes."

"What sort of music does this thing have?"

"Name it. We have all selections."

"Anything but love songs or sad songs about romance."

With that, Dave pushed a few buttons and hard rock 'n roll filled the car.

"Yes!" Julie grinned and pumped her fist out in front of her.

Settling back into her seat, Julie knew that she would come out of this all right.

Not necessarily unscathed, but all right.

Chapter Two

THE TURKS AND CAICOS ISLANDS

By the time Julie's plane finally landed at the Providenciales International Airport, all of the surprising and various emotions that she'd encountered during the flight had faded into a blessed numbness.

First, there had been the empty seat next to her. A constant reminder of her husbandless status.

It wasn't so much that she was missing Spencer. It was more the fact that the seat was supposed to have been filled by a husband.

And then the tears had started to quietly fall.

Second, the stress and toll of the day had finally hit her like a brick.

Okay, the champagne from the limo and the second glass from the flight attendant hadn't helped either.

Julie woke up about three hours into the flight with a stiff neck and a mouth that felt like it had been pasted shut.

Julie had surreptitiously looked around the plane's first-class cabin to see if anyone had noticed her sleeping.

Nope, no eye contact from anyone.

Wait ... here came the flight attendant with a tray.

For her.

With a damp warm washcloth.

Yep, someone had noticed.

Julie had thanked the attendant for the washcloth and had decided to just wipe all that Broadway makeup off.

When she'd finished with the first washcloth, she'd had to ask the attendant for a second one.

There were two false eyelashes hanging on the first one.

When the second cloth was brought to her, along with a small mirror, Julie had realized her mistake.

There had been layers upon layers of various shading, shadowing, and lining of the eyes and lips that she'd barely made a dent in.

So, she decided to use the second cloth to just clean up the smears a little.

It had taken her a while to get it right, but she was pleased with the results.

Then her mind had gone to where this had all started.

Julie was so happy for her friend, Kristy.

Kristy's wedding to her long-time fiancée, Jackson, was just perfect.

The weather was a cool 70 degrees with just the slightest of breezes.

The outdoor setting was placed beneath the shade of several tall oak trees whose branches intertwined above the small gathering.

The bride was stunningly beautiful.

And for the first time in history, Julie's bridesmaid's dress was flattering and COULD be used more than once.

As one of the bridesmaids, Julie felt sophisticated and elegant standing at the altar, watching Cate, the Maid of Honor, hold Kristy's bouquet while Kristy exchanged vows with Jackson.

The small gathering included family from both sides, several friends from where Jackson worked, Cate's on-again, off-again boyfriend, Dr. Derek Coburn, as well as a handful of friends who pretty much made up the rest of the wedding party.

At the reception, Julie and Cate had given a toast to the bride and groom, which seemed to go over well.

Julie had told a funny story about all the bridal magazines Kristy had made Jackson look at.

When Cate added her own story of the couple, Julie smiled at the evident closeness between the two sisters Cate and Kristy.

After the toast ended with a slightly off-color story, Julie watched Cate and her doctor exchange a personal glance that sent the room temperature up a couple of degrees.

As far as Cate's love life, Julie thought back to one of the many phone calls she'd gotten from Cate a few months ago, asking for advice on how to get the handsome young doctor to notice her.

From what Julie could gather from Cate's comments, the doctor had already noticed her, but there was something standing in the way.

Julie's first suggestion of showing up at the ER where he worked with some sort of non-specific physical complaint didn't seem like the right thing to Cate.

So, Julie had finally told her, "Just show up at the end of his shift. Offer to buy him a cup of coffee."

And that's exactly what Cate had done.

And here they were now at Kristy and Jackson's wedding, at the moment a couple.

When it came time for Kristy to toss her bouquet, Julie gathered with the others, not really intending to even try to catch it. Yet, somehow that darn bunch of flowers landed smack dab in her hands.

Which led Julie to start thinking about her own biological clock and the absence of any husband in sight.

Which led her to start going out with her boss, after he had persisted in getting her to agree to a date.

Which led to Julie and Spencer getting engaged.

Which led to where she was now.

❦

When the plane touched down on the runway at the Providenciales International Airport, Julie thought she had pulled it all together pretty well.

Right up until she caught a glimpse of herself in the mirror in the women's restroom on the concourse where she'd headed right after disembarking.

Who was that bedraggled, worn-out woman staring back at her? A far cry from the bride in the mirror earlier that day.

Wow. Had it only been that morning?

Julie grimaced at the thought, gave a big sigh, and headed out of the restroom and towards the baggage and customs area.

Almost two hours later, Julie was finally able to climb into a cab and was on her way to the Honeymoon Suite at the Regency Hotel.

Well, this should be awkward.

Or exhilarating.

Or depressing.

Maybe all three.

The clerk at the front desk was an angel. He made sure Julie's luggage was swiftly taken to her room.

He didn't bat an eye when Julie announced it would only be herself in the room.

In fact, he made it seem like that was the norm.

Yep, he was an angel; one with excellent public relations skills.

When Julie finally closed the suite's door, it took her a minute to realize that there was a huge, glass-enclosed, walk-in shower actually located smack dab in the middle between the two rooms; it opened to the bedroom and had a glass wall that faced the sitting room.

To Julie, it was one of most ridiculous amenities ever offered by any hotel.

She supposed the magnificent shower thing was romantic and sexy for some.

But without a romantic partner, it was just sort of captivating – in an odd sort of way.

Luckily, there was a second full bathroom with a door that closed.

Julie slipped off her shoes and started unpacking her luggage.

The two gorgeous new dresses that she had packed for evenings out at a bar or restaurant were now hung on padded hangers in one of the two closets.

The new gossamer-thin teddy was tossed into one of the bottom drawers.

Ditto with the new lacy underwear and matching bra sets.

Julie mentally patted herself on the back for also packing the clothes she lived in every day. Comfy pants and jeans, casual tops, cotton underwear, everyday bras, slip-on tennies, etc.

When she finished unpacking everything, she helped herself to an orange from the fruit and flower bowl that had been a welcoming gift from the hotel.

Thank goodness there hadn't been any tacky bride and groom greeting card or wedding things included.

Or, maybe that front desk clerk had made them disappear before she got to her room.

Either way, she was thankful.

Julie took the orange out onto the room's balcony which overlooked the ocean.

It was a stunning view!

The saltwater smelled great.

The breeze was cool.

The lounge chair was super comfortable.

Julie sat back and ate her orange, too tired to think.

A phone was ringing.

Julie frowned.

Someone needed to get it.

It was still ringing.

Julie opened her eyes and it took a moment for her to register where she was.

In that split-second moment before she remembered, there was a quiet span of no worries.

And then the truth set in.

The phone in her hotel room was ringing.

Julie jumped up from the lounge chair where she'd fallen asleep, ran inside to the phone, and answered.

"Hello?" Her voice was slightly breathless from the small sprint.

"Julie?"

What the heck!

"Spencer? Why are you calling?"

"Baby, I just wanted to say again how sorry I am."

Spencer's voice truly sounded remorseful.

Julie just stood there with the phone to her ear and her mouth hanging open.

A moment passed.

"Baby?" Spencer's voice was reticent.

Another moment passed.

Finally, Julie found her voice, "Did you just call me 'Baby?'"

Now it was Spencer's turn to be silent.

"I said, did you just call me 'Baby?'"

Julie's voice had taken on a tone of disbelief.

"Well, yes. I, I did."

"Don't."

"Mmmm. Okay?"

"Spencer, why did you call? I'm busy."

Julie hoped her voice sounded a bit bored.

"Busy! With what?"

"None of your business. I'm hanging up now. Do not call me again."

Julie didn't sound angry, just certain.

19

And she hung up the phone.

She stood there for a couple of minutes, waiting to see if he called back.

Finally, shaking her head in disbelief, she went into the bathroom and washed the sticky orange peel residue from her hands.

Then she wiped the phone, too.

The nap had been wonderful. She felt rejuvenated.

She glanced at the clock next to the bed and realized it was dinner time.

She took a quick shower (in the closed-door bathroom, thankyouverymuch), and put on some slacks and a Caribbean Blue blouse, with some jeweled sandals on her newly manicured feet.

Heading down to the lobby, Julie started to think about what she was going to do while here in the islands.

"Miss Julie!" The receptionist cheerfully called out her name as she crossed the lobby area.

Julie turned to him, smiling. His happiness was contagious.

"Miss Julie, I have saved our best table for you." And with that he motioned to the steward who stood at the door to the Regency's restaurant on the other side of the lobby.

The steward smiled and waved Julie over to where he stood. "Please follow me, Miss Julie."

It only took a moment for Julie to realize that the hotel receptionist and the steward were NOT pointing out her unmarried status.

It was just the way she was being addressed.

Maybe they weren't certain what her last name was supposed to be.

Either way, Julie didn't find it disconcerting. In fact, it was very nice, especially with the smiles that were attached to the greetings.

Sure enough, they had saved the best table for her and it was perfect.

It was a window table behind a potted palm that gave her a modicum of privacy without being cut off from the rest of the dining room.

The view of the ocean was spectacular. The sun had just gone down over the horizon and the sunset was a blaze of red, orange, pink, and a touch of azure blue.

Soothing and sensational at the same time.

The waiter took her drink order, which appeared in front of her almost immediately.

Sipping the cocktail, Julie grimaced and realized she actually wanted something non-alcoholic; she was still getting over the champagne.

Julie was not usually a drinker of more than one beer, or under Spencer's tutelage, one glass of expensive wine.

The waiter immediately handled her new request and she found herself with a huge glass of fruited iced tea which hit the spot.

Just as she heard her stomach growl, the waiter appeared with her salad and a basket of fresh baked breads with a side of whipped butter in a beautiful small cut-glass dish.

Julie dug in with gusto.

For the past two weeks she'd been starving herself to make sure she fit into the wedding dress.

She wasn't even aware when the waiter replaced her empty drink glass with a new full one.

At the precise moment her salad plate was empty, the entrée appeared in its place.

The seafood was fresh, and the vegetables were pan-seared with butter and an herb that was exactly right. She slowed down and started to think about what her next steps would be.

They had scheduled (scratch that; actually, **she'd** done all the planning) for tomorrow with a fishing boat that would take them out for a couple of days; deep sea fishing for Spencer.

None for Julie. She was just going to enjoy the boat, the sea, and the lack of phones and schedules.

Julie still thought that sounded like a great idea. Take two days off on the open ocean. No worries, no problems, just fresh air, open skies and an e-reader full of new books.

Sounded perfect.

Chapter Three

AYE AYE, CAPTAIN!

The next morning, bright and early, Julie took a taxi to the *TnT Charter Boats* dock.

She had expected the driver to take her only a block or two north to the main cruise ship dock. Instead he took her southeast along Beetham Highway.

It seemed to Julie that they were heading inland, not towards the sea.

Suddenly, the driver took a fast hard right and drove them down a small asphalt drive that was dwarfed between towering warehouses the entire length of the road.

At the very end of the drive was an old wharf.

At the tip of that wharf was a pristine white 75-foot Mikelson boat.

The only reason Julie knew the name of that type of boat was because of the research she'd done to hire this particular one.

And this one sold for the hefty price of at least two million dollars, without all the bells and whistles.

The owner had shelled out a lot of cash for this beauty.

Spencer had been looking at purchasing one and had decided they could use part of their honeymoon to "test drive" his future toy.

The driver dropped Julie off with her smallest piece of luggage plus a large tote bag.

She'd decided to leave the remainder of her things at the hotel, since the reservation was for two weeks and had already been paid for.

The wharf looked deserted this morning. No sound from anywhere. She walked to the end of the pier and stood next to the boat.

"Hello!"

Julie waited.

No answer.

"Anyone there?"

Julie waited again.

No answer again.

Well, this is great. No way to call a taxi, since she'd left her phone back at the hotel, looking forward to a couple of days unplugged. Now what?

Wait. What was that?

She heard noises of some sort coming from the boat. Someone was on board.

Well, no time like the present.

Julie climbed onto the boat with her two bags and stood on the deck at the back of the boat.

Looking around, her nose wrinkled slightly at the number of empty beer cans littered around a low table and settee area. Empty chip bags also dotted the ground while adding nothing to the décor.

She heard more noises that sounded like they were coming from the area above and in front of her. She looked at the set of stairs leading up to that area.

And watched as first a pair of manly feet in scruffy deck shoes started down the stairs.

The feet were followed shortly by a pair of chiseled legs with just the right amount of soft bleached hair.

Next came a pair of cut-off shorts sitting very low on a pair of masculine slim hips.

After that it was a bare torso and wide chest that nearly stopped her breath.

The broad neck that was supporting the square-jawed face tensed when Julie figured he'd finally spotted her standing there.

Strong hands reached up and removed sunglasses just as his feet hit the deck.

"Who are you and what are you doing on my boat?"

Julie was stunned by the angry greeting and took a small step back.

Then she quickly remembered that this was the start of her new life being the new Julie.

So, after a split second, she decided to show no fear and stepped forward again.

Just as she was about to tell the man exactly who she was and why she was there, a mermaid started to arise out of a hole in the deck that Julie hadn't noticed before.

Said mermaid was tall, lithe, and perfectly proportioned – if you were Miss America or a movie star.

As the vision made it all the way up through the deck, Julie noted that there wasn't a tail, just long legs that didn't quit – something Julie wished she had.

Come to think of it, Julie was about as tall as those legs. Sigh.

Julie also noticed that it looked like the beauty was wearing last night's party clothes and carrying her four-inch heels in one hand.

The man who had just verbally accosted Julie for being there, solicitously offered a hand to the beauty.

The beauty wrapped an arm around his neck and gave him a kiss on the cheek before turning to leave, saying, "Thank you, Zan. That was just what I needed."

She smiled sweetly at Julie as she passed her while leaving the boat.

Julie could do nothing but just stare after her as she gracefully stepped onto the dock just as a taxi arrived for her.

Julie continued to watch as the woman slid into the back seat of the taxi, waving and smiling at the man on the boat just before she closed the door behind her.

"I said, who are you and what are you doing on my boat?"

Julie had just about had it with the bad customer service.

She'd paid a fortune for this charter!

If this was how this company worked, she was going to get a refund.

"I'm your charter for this weekend. Could I please speak to the captain?"

Silence.

The infuriating man just stood there staring at her.

Julie tried to keep her composure under his unrelenting stare.

Finally, the man dropped his eyes from her and took a deep breath while raking a hand through his tousled hair.

"You're speaking to him."

"What?"

"You're speaking to him. I'm the captain."

What in the heck had she gotten herself into?

Julie couldn't even think. This was bizarre.

When she'd originally called to set up the charter, the man she'd spoken with was very courteous, friendly, and business-like.

Now, looking around the deck, seeing all the empty beer cans, she felt like she'd made a very bad choice.

She saw the man (was his name Zan?) follow along the path that her eyes had just travelled, picking up the empty cans and putting them into a trash container next to the table.

He rapidly cleaned up the area and turned to address Julie.

She stiffened a little, waiting for whatever the next barrage of communication from him was going to be.

"You must be Mrs. Prendergast."

"No. I'm Ms. Anderson. Mr. Prendergast was unable to make it."

Now it was Zan's turn to pause, while he tried to figure it out.

"Oh. Okay. Is there a Mrs. Prendergast?"

"No. That would have been me if the wedding had taken place."

Julie had no idea why she felt compelled to answer any personal questions, but she continued to tell him.

"The honeymoon trip has been cancelled, but I'm using the reservations for a well-earned vacation, which is what I need now that Mr. Prendergast decided to boff my best friend and maid of honor."

"He did both of them?"

Zan couldn't help the response he blurted out.

That Mr. Prendergast felt he had the right to cheat on his future bride with, not only her best friend but also with her maid of honor?

That took some blind stupidity on the man's part. Or some huge ...

"What? NO! No. Charlotte is – was my best friend and also my maid of honor."

Julie knew she sounded a bit wounded.

"Oh! ... Oh. ... Well. ... It's still not right."

For some reason, Zan's simple statement made Julie feel so much better.

"No, it's not right."

They both gave a small smile to the other and shared the understanding in the moment.

The sound of someone else coming up the hole in the deck broke the spell.

"Zan! Uncle Zan! Why are you shouting? I just got to bed a couple of hours ago and could really use some quiet."

Julie caught the eye roll that Zan did before drawing in his breath and speaking to the young man who had joined them on deck.

"Robert, this is one of our charter clients for the next two days."

The young man turned and looked at Julie. His bloodshot eyes lit up a little as he scanned her from head to toe and back up again.

"Robert! Knock it off."

Turning to Julie, Zan added, "I'm so sorry Ms. Anderson. My older sister sent her son to me for some shaping up, and he's still in his first week."

"And you allow him to drink and mess up your boat?" Julie knew she sounded like a prudish spinster but couldn't seem to hide her embarrassment from the creepy once-over she'd just received from the younger male.

"Robert, go back to bed and I'll get with you later."

Robert huffed like a 14-year-old, instead of the 21-year-old he was and headed back down the stairs.

"Ms. Anderson. I don't know what to say except to offer you a full refund. I'll, of course, pay for your taxi back to your hotel."

For some odd reason, Julie didn't want to go back to her hotel. She really wanted the open sea and fresh air. But, if she was using her ability to reason, she would accept a check and a ride back. Instead, she even surprised herself a little.

"Captain Zan, if that's how I'm supposed to address you, I've paid for two days on the open sea. I have no intention of fishing. I just want to have two days of uneventful sleeping, eating, and reading everything on my Kindle. Can that be done?"

Zan was sure he could deliver that request.

"Ms. Anderson, I can almost guarantee peace and quiet. Even if I have to tie Robert up and keep him in his room. May I carry your bags to your room?" Zan reached out a hand towards her luggage in a gesture of 'May I?'

It was a gallant gesture and Julie sort of melted at it.

"Yes, you may. And please call me Julie."

"Okay, Julie. Follow me."

Julie's cabin was one of three guest suites located downstairs.

Was the correct term "below deck?" Julie thought to herself.

It had its own in-suite bathroom and a queen bed which looked super soft and comfortable.

The walls of her room were dark wood paneling that shone like it had just been polished. The nautical theme of the room was subdued and restful.

Yep, this was going to be perfect.

"After you get unpacked, I'll introduce you to the remainder of the crew and the other passengers, when they arrive, which should be any minute."

"Thank you. The suite is perfect." Julie's smile did something to Zan's heart. This was one brave little gal. She seemed to be taking everything pretty well, including his awful greeting to her.

"If you have any questions at all, just yell for me. I'm not far away – at least never more than 75 feet." Zan smiled at his own inside joke.

Julie returned the smile and watched him while he left the suite, gently closing the door behind him. Maybe this was going to be a very restful trip after all. Just what she needed.

Julie felt hopeful, right up until she was introduced to the second passenger on this trip.

He was loud, brash, and obviously a very important person ... somewhere.

His perpetual one-sided grin was frozen in place by the cigar clamped between his side teeth.

The cigar only came out of his mouth when he was making a point, holding the thick, brown, slightly moist object between two fingers while he punctuated the sky with it.

Luckily his attendant (Personal Assistant? Man Servant? Accessory?) seemed to be a nice man in his mid-30's who didn't seem to mind his boss at all.

His name was Marc. Julie figured he must be being paid very well for him to put up with the rudeness directed at him whenever Mr. VIP barked an order.

Lunch was definitely an interesting meal. Only one person spoke – Mr. VIP – while everyone else was forced to just sit and listen.

After one of Mr. VIP's rants about something, Julie glanced over at Zan at the same time he glanced at her. The shared buried mirth in their eyes made the meal more palatable for both of them.

Julie had now met Captain Zan, Mr. VIP, Mr. VIP's assistant Marc, Zan's nephew, Robert, and the third crew member who was also the cook.

Julie wasn't quite sure about him yet. He was quiet, efficient, and could prepare plain good food. His name was Pierre and when Julie had asked him, he said he came from Somalia.

When he spoke English, there was a different slight accent that Julie couldn't quite place. Sort of like maybe he'd also lived in France or India or maybe even Scotland at some point in his life.

The hour after lunch consisted of a tour of the boat by Zan, as well as covering the protocol regarding the almost non-existent rare event where they would have to abandon the ship while at sea.

There was a small covered motorboat secured on the back of the top deck that everyone would be able to fit into along with several water containers and emergency supplies.

Of course, Mr. VIP expressed a somewhat crude remark when Zan showed them all how to put on the life vests in case of an emergency.

"We used to call those sweet little items Mae Wests when I was in the service. You know, because of Mae's voluptuous figure."

Julie would have been fine with his remark, except that he looked directly at her chest when he stated it.

Of course, she was immediately uncomfortable with his remark, but wasn't quite sure how to handle it.

It turned out she didn't have to do anything.

Zan immediately stepped in between Mr. VIP and Julie while starting to put away the vests.

None of the other men joined VIP in his laughter at his own joke. In fact, they each acted as though they had not even heard the remark.

It was the closest thing to a 'direct cut' that Julie had ever witnessed. It also put her very much at ease.

"Let's head to the back of the boat and I'll show you the fishing set up." Zan's voice sounded so calm and matter of fact. Julie was more than happy to look at a "fishing set up," whatever that was.

Mr. VIP was very impressed with what the boat offered and had tons of questions that to Julie sounded like a foreign language.

While Zan continued to answer Mr. VIP's questions, Julie slipped away to look for a spot where she'd be able to relax and read.

She climbed up a set of stairs which led to the top deck.

At the front of that deck, just below the windows of what looked like the cockpit (or whatever the nautical term was for where you drive the boat from) there was a small area with two chaise lounge chairs.

The pads on the chairs perfectly matched the rest of the boat's nautical theme. They were made of a soft canvas with leather piping around the edges.

Julie decided to give one of the chairs a test ride and stretched out on it. The sun was not directly on her, there was a light breeze, and it seemed the perfect place for her to read while on the trip.

Pretty soon, she heard and felt the engines start up and the boat moved slowly away from the island and out towards open sea. The view from where she was sitting was perfect!

The breeze, the clean ocean smell, and the vibration from the boat's engines lulled Julie into a semi-sleep twilight state that felt so relaxing.

"May I join you?"

The male voice was unexpected and gave Julie a slight start.

She opened her eyes, shading them with one hand.

It was Marc, Mr. VIP's assistant.

She looked up at him and gave him a shrug and a slight smile.

"Of course. It's a free ship."

"Thank you." Marc stretched out on the other lounge chair.

After settling in, crossing his ankles, and heaving a deep sigh, he turned his head to face Julie.

"I'm sorry about earlier."

Julie realized he was referring to the uncomfortable comment made by his employer.

"Oh, please. Don't worry about it. Besides, you didn't say it. He did."

Julie wished their conversation would move onto something more neutral.

"I know. Sometimes he can be a bit much."

Julie turned her head towards Marc and raised an eyebrow. "Sometimes?"

Marc laughed. "Okay. Most of the time."

They were both laughing when Zan entered the main bridge which was located just above and behind where Julie and Marc were stretched out on the lounge chairs.

Zan had taken the boat out to sea from the open top bridge, which was his favorite haunt during a sail.

Once out to sea, he'd decided to steer from the lower bridge, which was enclosed.

In fact, he wanted to find Julie and ask her if she wanted to see the bridge and maybe steer the boat for a few minutes, since there was no traffic out here at the moment.

Zan spotted Julie and Marc on the lounge deck just below, seeming to be very chummy and was surprised at his reaction.

At first he was unable to recognize it. If anyone had asked him, he would have denied it vehemently.

When had he ever felt even a smidge of jealousy? Not with his ex-fiancé.

Certainly not with his few ex-girlfriends.

In fact, he took great pride in the fact that he'd never felt possessive towards any relationship.

And now, out of the blue, he actually felt something that he didn't enjoy at all.

Also, it didn't make any sense to him why he'd feel this towards a woman he'd just met a few hours ago.

He didn't like it. In fact, it made him angry and uncomfortable.

Stepping out of the bridge and down the short two steps onto the lounge deck, he walked over to the couple.

The frown on his face was unexpected and both Marc and Julie noticed it.

"Is my boss causing trouble?"

Marc was already up out of the lounge chair and at the ready to head off and handle whatever it was that needed handling.

"What? No."

Zan could hear his voice but didn't seem to be able to have any control over it.

He sounded miffed.

"Captain Zan?" Julie could see that he was upset and wanted to help, if possible. "What is it?"

Now Zan felt like a deer in the headlights.

He froze.

He'd never encountered this feeling before and really, truly didn't like it at all.

"Nothing. It's nothing." He was able to make his tone a little less abrasive.

"Marc, how do you like your accommodations? Are they sufficient for you? I know it's the smallest of the three suites."

Zan also just now realized that Marc's suite was right next to Julie's.

Was that a growl that came out of his throat?

Zan coughed to cover the sound.

"The room is great. I really like it. Thank you."

Marc was still trying to figure out why the captain seemed out of sorts.

"And yours, Miss Anderson? Is it sufficient?"

Zan hated how he sounded. So stiff and well, disgruntled.

So, he tried to add a smile at the end of his question.

Unfortunately, it looked more like a grimace.

What has gotten into this man? Maybe he's more unhinged than Julie had first thought.

Maybe this trip was a bad decision.

Too late now. They were at sea.

Unless Julie wanted a long swim in possibly shark-infested waters, she was sort of trapped if something were to happen.

Thank goodness, Marc seemed to have a stable head on his shoulders. Maybe she'd stay closer to him if necessary – when he wasn't waiting on his boss.

Julie realized that she'd gotten lost in her thoughts.

Both men were staring at her. Zan with that frown on his brow and Marc with a slightly amused half smile on his face.

"Um. I'm sorry. I phased out a little there. What was the question?"

"Is your room sufficient for your needs?" Zan wished with everything he had that he would just chill out and act normal.

So far, this charter was rapidly becoming one of his least favorite ones.

"Yes. Thank you, Captain. It's perfect."

Julie really had no idea what was going on with this strange man.

"Good."

Silence.

Awkward silence.

"Was there anything else?" Marc seemed very amused at whatever was going on, as though he was in on a joke that Julie had not yet caught on to.

Zan was able to pull himself together finally.

"Yes! I was wondering if either of you would like to come up to the bridge and maybe pilot the boat for a little bit. I like to offer all my guests the chance to captain this beauty."

Zan's smile was authentic when he talked about his boat.

Marc looked over at Julie and raised his brows in question.

Julie looked back and nodded yes.

Zan let out a breath that he didn't know he'd been holding.

"Please follow me." He turned and went up the two steps and into the enclosed bridge area.

He made it to the front windows just in time to see Marc standing next to Julie's lounge chair, holding out a hand to help her up.

Jeez Louise! What the heck was wrong with him?

For Pete's sake, back down for a second. Just take a breath. Ease up.

By the time Julie and Marc entered the cockpit area, Zan was almost back to normal.

He'd given this tour often enough that his words came out easy and he was able to give his usual basic introduction to the various levers, dials, and gauges.

The view this high up on the boat was always spectacular and Zan knew just how much it usually impressed his guests.

Both Julie and Marc truly enjoyed steering the boat for a short while each. After about ten minutes, Zan got a call on the intercom.

Mr. VIP was looking for Marc.

"I hope to see you after dinner." Marc's smile at Julie was sincere and friendly.

Julie returned the smile.

"I'd like that." Julie felt a little like maybe she'd found a new friend.

She was certainly not looking for any sort of new relationship.

Marc turned and hurried down to the Lanai deck at the back of the boat, where his boss was.

For about a minute, neither Zan nor Julie spoke.

"Look. I'm sorry about the way this trip has started off for you." Zan was glad his voice was almost back to normal.

"I'm also sorry about your non-wedding. That can't have been easy."

Julie was suddenly surprised at the rush of heat to her eyes and the tears that started welling up.

They embarrassed her now.

She hadn't cried at the church.

She hadn't cried in the limo.

In fact, she hadn't felt much at all.

Well, except for that interesting bout on the airplane – but we weren't counting that, were we?

And now here, some newly met man offers a handful of comforting words and she becomes a weeping ball of melt-down?

Neither of them knew exactly how it happened.

Maybe Zan had reached for her at the same time Julie had turned into his arms.

Either way, they fit perfectly and Zan held her gently while she cried out every last pent up tear.

In actual fact, she soaked his shirt.

When the episode finally wound down, they just stood there feeling very comfortable.

It felt natural.

Julie slowly became aware of Zan's hand gently rubbing her back up and down.

It was such a calming feeling.

A sigh escaped from her, followed immediately by a hiccup.

"I'm sorry, but I'm afraid I ruined your shirt." Julie was surprised that she wasn't more embarrassed.

"That's okay. Sometimes you just need a cathartic release."

Julie paused for a moment, pulled back, and looked up into Zan's face.

"Cathartic?" A smile twitched her lips.

It surprised her to see a blush creep up Zan's neck onto his face.

"Um. Too poetic?" Zan didn't have a clue where that word had come from. It wasn't like he used it often. In fact, this time was pretty much the one and only time that word had ever come out of his mouth.

Julie smiled as she pulled away.

"The word is perfect."

"Are you feeling better?"

Zan's face held such concern that Julie almost teared up again.

As though he knew that's what was about to happen, he looked down at his shirt with an exaggerated look of horror; and in his best prissy voice asked, "Oh no! How will I ever get this out?"

Julie's choked laugh came out sounding a little like a sob.

When she saw Zan's face take on a look of "uh-oh!" she waved her hands in front of her face to show she was fine.

Between the gesture and the smile on her face, Zan knew she was going to be all right.

Zan didn't know if he liked the sudden flip flop in his heart or not.

As Julie asked a question about one of the gauges on the bridge, he tucked that thought away for now.

He knew he'd bring it out later that night and look at it.

Not because he wanted to, but because it wouldn't allow itself to be ignored.

Chapter Four

TESTOSTERONE OVERLOAD AND CHEST BEATING

What was it about men, anyway?

Julie had decided by mid-morning the next day that she'd never understand men and what made them click.

One minute, she and Zan were best friends and able to talk freely and easily.

Then she has a conversation with Marc, who, by-the-way, has been acting very strangely; like he knew a secret that no one else knew.

Although Marc seemed very flirty with her, Julie knew he wasn't truly interested. She just didn't get that vibe from him.

He had been pretending to be interested in something she was looking at over the side of the boat and had put his arm around her back, as though he was protecting her. Whatever.

And then right after that, they'd run into Zan and he wouldn't even look at her, much less converse in any sort of friendly manner.

'Miss Anderson?' Where had that come from? One minute she's 'Julie' or 'Jules' and thirty minutes later, Zan is back to being all professional and formal with her.

Nope. Julie just didn't understand.

All she wanted to do now was stretch out on the lounge chair and finish reading her new Jude Deveraux book. A tall cool drink would be nice, too.

At that precise moment, Pierre appeared as though summoned, carrying a tray with a pink frothy concoction complete with umbrella and pineapple chunk.

"How did you know that was exactly what I wanted!" Julie smiled at the mostly silent man.

He just bowed towards her so she could take the glass off the tray. His facial expression was pleasant, but he remained silent.

"Thank you! I really appreciate this." Julie smiled again, hoping for a "you're welcome!"

Pierre just gave a nod and silently walked away, heading down the stairs that led to the salon/galley area.

Julie watched him leave.

Men! She just shook her head.

Drawing a sip through the pretty straw, Julie decided that Pierre could be as silent as he wanted. This was the most delicious drink she'd ever had. She knew it must have some rum in it, but it just tasted fruity and gentle and it went down so smoothly.

This was heaven. A book, a drink, the ocean, blue sky ...

Julie wasn't sure how long she'd been asleep. The sun seemed lower in the sky. There were some clouds slowly moving in, threatening rain. A slight chill brought goose bumps to her arms.

She got up and stretched. For the first time in a very long time, Julie felt totally relaxed and calm. Yep, the ocean and a good book, and all problems go away.

Gathering up her Kindle, she looked around for the drink glass. It wasn't there. Obviously, someone had come and collected it while she was napping. At that realization, she was very glad that she was wearing capri's and a large loose top instead of her bathing suit. That would have been a little bit creepy.

Zan knew he shouldn't have been staring at Julie while she slept. It was just so easy to watch her while guiding the boat from the bridge through the semi-calm waters. He would catch himself looking at her legs and then he would throw his attention out to the ocean. Only to have his eyes slowly move back to her, stretched out on the lounge chair.

When Pierre came back up to fetch the empty drink glass, he'd glanced up to the bridge and saw Zan. Pierre nodded at Zan and went back to the galley area with the empty glass. Zan had acknowledged Pierre with a single nod. He was a good employee. Although he'd only been with Zan for a few months, Pierre had proven himself to be a hard worker and a better-than-okay cook. He wasn't much of a conversationalist, nor did he pal around with Zan's nephew or any of the many guests who had come and gone.

Now Zan's eyes once again followed the path of least resistance. What was it about this woman that captured his attention? Yes, she was beautiful, but he knew lots of beautiful women and none of them had ever created this effect in him.

In fact, Zan usually had society women throwing themselves at him. Especially at the fundraising events he was so frequently invited to.

Zan's full name was Alexander Roland DeKeurge. THE Alexander Roland DeKeurge. Second generation philanthropist, eligible bachelor, heir to a fortune, and all-around nice guy. His family had been one of the founding families in the Caribbean when the Dutch had first arrived generations ago.

The charter boat gig was how he relaxed and got away from all the "high-society" stuff. It was nice being treated as just another regular guy.

From his earliest memories, he'd always attended those events with his parents, as he was being groomed to take over the company business. For years while growing up, he'd protested the built-in adoration from fawning matrons with young daughters.

It was a bit much.

The charter boat business kept him sane and grounded. In fact, he wanted to grow the business into being the best in the industry.

Now, here he was actually interested in a woman who had no intention of getting involved at the moment.

His timing was, as usual, lacking.

Oh, he'd had plenty of dates with various women. As well as two serious relationships that hadn't panned out. And one ex-fiancée who he tried unsuccessfully to keep buried from his thoughts.

And now his parents were pressuring him to settle down in the company.

His father wanted him to take over the family business completely. Not just show up for the requisite philanthropic events to hand out large donation checks on behalf of his family.

Zan still hadn't fully made up his mind about that yet. He kept postponing that decision.

He loved the amount of good that his family's money allowed them to do. He just didn't know if he wanted to be embroiled full time in the day-to-day running of the empire. Sitting in an office wasn't his idea of a pleasant work environment.

He felt at home when at sea.

Sailing on the ocean had been his passion since he'd captained his first small sailboat at the age of eight. Zan was a natural and had caught on fast. As he grew up, so did the boats he captained.

Unfortunately, his father had not shared his enthusiasm. From an early age, Zan had understood that someday, as the only son, he would be required to fill his father's shoes as head of the family business.

Zan had tried several times, unsuccessfully, to get his parents to turn the reins over to his sister, Jaimee.

She was the one who had the drive and the ambition to run it. She was business smart and truly enjoyed the office environment. In fact, she thrived on it.

Born Rebecca Jaimyson DeKeurge, she was a force to behold. Beautiful, business-brilliant, with unstoppable energy that made Zan tired just to watch. It didn't matter whether it was 6:00 am at an early meeting or 9:00 pm at a formal fundraiser, Jaimee was always on top and in control; making it all look so easy.

Unfortunately, their father didn't really see her as anything other than a temporary placeholder while Zan "worked through whatever he had to work through" before he took on the mantle of CEO.

Zan's wandering thoughts ended when Julie seemed to wake up, stand up, and stretch.

He couldn't take his eyes off her. Every movement was graceful and feminine. Her ex-fiancé must have been completely nuts.

Just then, Julie looked up and saw Zan. She smiled hesitantly at him.

He smiled back and gestured for her to come join him at the boat's bridge.

After just a moment of indecision, she headed up the stairs leading to where Zan was.

"Hi."

"Hi."

They just sort of stood there in a semi-comfortable silence, looking at each other.

Zan was the first one to break the silence.

"So, how are you enjoying the sail so far?"

"It's relaxing!"

"Are you having any difficulty with seasickness yet?"

"Surprisingly, no. I thought I would, but I feel fine."

"That's great."

"Yep."

And silence once again descended.

Silence until Marc popped his head up from the deck below.

"There you are, Julie!" His smile was megawatt.

Julie glanced between Zan, who had now turned toward the controls on the engine board appearing to read some gauges, and Marc who just stood down there grinning at her.

"Well, I guess I should let you get back to work."

"Yep. Guess you should."

Why did he have to sound so stilted? Julie couldn't figure out what she'd done wrong this time.

After a silent sigh, Julie went down the stairs to where Marc was now standing.

"Hi, Marc."

"Hi, Kiddo! Would you like to join me in the galley? I found a deck of cards and my boss is taking a nap, so I've got some free time. Do you like cards?"

Julie glanced back up to where Zan was apparently thoroughly engrossed in something or other.

Looking back at Marc, she replied, "You bet! Poker?"

Marc grinned even wider. "We'll play for pennies with a top bet of fifty cents?"

Julie laughed at his boyish charm. "Perfect. But prepare to leave the game broke."

Zan glanced down at them just in time to see Marc put a hand on the small of Julie's back as he guided her to the stairs leading to the galley.

After Julie descended, Marc turned towards Zan and did a small mock-salute of triumph.

Zan's mood got darker. It was going to be a long weekend Just not in the way Zan thought it would.

Chapter Five

DRAWN IN BY A TURTLE

The sun was just going down over the horizon when Pierre rang the dinner bell.

After a loud, rousing game of Five Card Stud, (which Julie won completely) Marc and Julie had retired to their separate suites at Pierre's urging to change for dinner.

Marc had paused outside Julie's door and had leaned an arm up against the wall next to her head as she leaned back against the door.

Marc leaned in a little closer and asked Julie, "Do you know the amazing thing I see when I look into your eyes?"

Julie felt herself blush at Marc's attention. It had been a very long time since she'd had a good-looking male's attention focused on her and her alone. His intense gaze glanced up the stairs for just a moment.

Marc moved in a little closer.

She was finding it a little hard to draw a breath, but managed to say "No, what?"

Just then, out of nowhere, Zan came down the steps to the quarters, stalked past them, and growled "Yourself?"

Julie didn't know what happened, but all of a sudden Marc stood up straight and threw back his head and laughed.

Zan made a growling noise and kept going into the crew quarters and out of sight.

As though nothing had happened before, Marc smiled at Julie and stated in a friendly voice, "See you at dinner, Jules!" He turned around and entered his suite door without a backwards glance.

Julie entered her own cabin, shaking her head in question. *What the heck was going on around here, anyway?*

Thirty minutes later, all the guests were gathered in the galley, seated at the large L-shaped dining table.

The feast in front of them smelled heavenly.

Pierre had certainly outdone himself, was the primary thought from Zan when he finally joined everyone after anchoring the boat so it wouldn't drift.

Julie looked great. Better than great. She was wearing a brightly colored plain cotton dress that looked like it was being held up by two thin tie-straps on each shoulder. Zan wondered how it might feel to untie them, one by one. To feel the smooth skin of her shoulders on his fingertips.

Where had that thought come from? Zan shook his head at his own imagination. Maybe he'd gotten too much sun that afternoon. That had to be it. It couldn't be that he was developing feelings for this woman who had entered his universe just one day ago. No way. And yet, he recalled the awful feeling of jealousy that had overtaken him when he had headed down the stairs to his cabin. Something about seeing Marc standing that close to Julie had bitten him. And he didn't like it.

The meal progressed mostly in silence, punctuated by murmurs of agreement that the food was delicious. Occasionally, Mr. VIP would tell a tale of one sort or another, but even he quieted down when no one seemed to be paying much attention to him.

Pierre had just served the desserts and various after-dinner drink choices when they all heard a ship's horn blasting from some distance away. Then they heard excited shouting float across the water.

Zan immediately moved to the top deck to check it all out and everyone followed.

Approximately 300 yards away, a small old fishing vessel was sitting still in the water. There were lights from the deck shining into the water, as though they were looking for something.

There was a net dragging next to the boat and the men on board were shouting and pointing at something in the net.

"We should head over there, don't you think? Maybe they need some help." Mr. VIP's statement carried to Zan's ears as everyone joined him on the deck to watch what was happening.

"No. We'll wait here." Zan felt that something just wasn't as it should be with the other vessel.

"What's in their net?" Zan's nephew chimed in.

"We'll wait here for now."

Julie could pick up on Zan's unease from something in his voice. However, that boat was small and the handful of people on it seemed truly upset over something.

"Maybe we should find out?"

Zan glanced over at Julie's question.

"No."

Julie thought his reply was harsh. Well, he didn't have to sound so put out. Julie crossed her arms.

Marc stepped over to her and placed an arm across her shoulders as though to comfort her. Zan's attention was so intent on the other boat that he didn't even notice Marc's movement towards Julie.

The people on Zan's boat stood there in silence like a frozen tableau, waiting for something to happen.

Just then, one of the men on the deck of the other boat jumped into the water next to the net. He then shouted excitedly at the others on deck.

"It's caught! I can't free it."

The remaining men on the deck strained towards the net, looking deeply into it and pointing excitedly.

"Aw. Common Uncle Zan. We need to help them." Robert's suggestion was seconded by several heads nodding in agreement.

"No." Zan wasn't about to try to explain everything that could be wrong with the present situation. His primary concern was keeping the people on his boat safe. As its captain, that was his primary job – the safety of those on his ship.

"Why are you being so hardheaded, Zan?"

Marc's question was delivered softer than it could have been.

Mr. VIP spoke up again.

"What could it hurt just to ask if they needed help?"

"I'm not comfortable with how this looks." Zan didn't feel that he owed anyone an explanation for his trepidation. Also, he wasn't used to people questioning his decisions. Maybe that was wrong of him, but at the moment it was not his primary concern; his attention being fully on the developing scene.

They certainly looked like they needed help, but something just didn't ring true to him.

He hadn't heard about any recent pirating happening in the Turks and Caicos area, but he didn't want to take any chances.

Just then the man who had jumped into the water shouted over to Zan's boat.

"Help! We can't get the turtle untangled from the net!"

"Uncle Zan! It's a turtle! We have to help, don't we?" Robert insisted.

Zan knew that the Hawksbill turtle was on the endangered species list. In fact, one of the last checks he had presented on behalf of his family's company was one for almost half a million to help with their preservation.

He still did not feel good about the other boat's intentions, but he also knew that he hadn't been on his game for this whole weekend. Maybe he was just overreacting. Damn, he hated it when he second guessed himself. It never seemed to end well.

Zan turned to look at the others. Their eyes were bouncing between looking at Zan and the other boat. It was Julie's look of pleading that made up his mind. If she hadn't been watching him so intently, he could have possibly held his ground. He just wanted her to stop looking at him in disbelief like he could be so cruel.

Still feeling uncomfortable, Zan reluctantly decided to pull up anchor and offer their help with saving the turtle. He knew his mom would have his head on a platter if she ever found out that he had refused to help one of their pet projects because he wasn't feeling like it.

"Okay. Let me get the anchor up."

Everyone else started smiling, which seemed to alleviate some of his disquiet.

Sort of.

He called down to the galley from the bridge, letting Pierre know they were moving. Zan then began pulling up the anchor with Robert's help. It was one of the few things his nephew had learned to do efficiently since arriving on the ship. After a very short time, but what seemed to be forever to the others, Zan started up the motors.

A happy cheer from the other boat reached his ears, which helped to alleviate his concerns a little.

As he closed the distance between the boats, he could see a little better into the net. Sure enough, there was a turtle caught in it. Okay, maybe this was legit.

But as he got even closer, the hair on the back of his neck stood up. Something was amiss. All of the people on the other deck had stopped cheering and were standing in readiness for something; watching and waiting.

All at once, Zan knew with complete certainty that the turtle in the net was a ruse. He swiveled towards his guests to warn them to take cover. But he was too late. Robert had already thrown a line over to the other boat, which was immediately secured to one of their larger cleats.

At the same time, one of the men threw a line over to Zan's boat with a military grade grappling hook on it which wedged itself into the deck around one of the rail posts.

Zan's stomach dropped at the same time his adrenaline kicked into overtime.

He had to protect everyone.

He had to protect Julie.

In a split second, he could tell from their faces that his guests had not yet conceived the danger they were in.

If they were lucky, they would only be put adrift, robbed of all their money and valuables.

If they were not, pain and suffering were imminent; especially for Julie, as the only female on board. He had to stop this now.

He looked around for Pierre but didn't see him anywhere. Finally, Marc happened to glance up at the bridge area and the smile melted away from his face. He could tell from Zan's expression that something was very wrong.

Zan lifted his chin towards Marc and he hurried up to the bridge to join Zan.

"It's a trick, isn't it?" Marc's words made it completely real for both of them.

Zan could only nod in affirmation.

"Julie." That single word from Zan was all Marc needed to move into action.

"Where?"

"There's a small hidden safe room built into the back of my cabin's closet. She should be able to hide there. It locks from the inside, and unless anyone knows it's there, it's invisible."

Marc didn't wait for further instructions. He smoothly dropped down onto the next deck where everyone was standing and took Julie's hand in his. He gently pulled her back away from the group.

She turned to Marc with a look of excitement on her face, thinking they were actually helping save the turtle. And just as Marc had reacted with Zan, her smile disappeared.

"What's wrong, Marc?"

At first, Julie thought Marc was in trouble because the expression on his face was so grim.

"I need you to come with me now. No questions. There's no time."

Julie felt a chill cover her back and arms at the intensity of Marc's words. She just stood there for a moment, not knowing what to do.

She turned and looked up at Zan in the bridge. He made a small intense motion for her to go with Marc.

She nodded once and turned back to Marc.

"Okay."

With that, Marc hurriedly lead her down to the crew quarters, keeping out of the line of sight of anyone else.

When they arrived at Zan's door, Marc didn't pause for a second. He drew Julie inside and closed the door.

"We're in danger, Jules. Especially you. Zan wants to safeguard you while we take care of this situation."

"But what's going on? I can help, I'm sure." Julie obviously hadn't grasped the situation yet.

Marc's look of concern was what let her know the degree of danger they were in.

"Jules. Being the only female on board, you're in greater danger than any of us guys. The men in the other boat will not be kind if they get their hands on you."

Her skin crawled with the realization of what Marc was saying.

She whooshed out a shaky breath and nodded her agreement and understanding.

"Good girl. Here we go." Marc went over to the closet and started feeling around the back panel for the opener. He used his fist to slam pressure on the right-hand side of it and it opened out towards him like a slender door; the hinges hidden in between the wood panels.

The space in the back of the closet was approximately the same length and height as the closet and about 3 feet deep. There was a soft-sided carryon bag on its floor. Marc did a quick inspection of the bag and found a flashlight, several bottles of water, some energy bars, and a cell phone.

He rapidly retrieved a pillow and blanket from Zan's bed while Julie moved into the space.

She turned towards Marc and received the pillow and blanket from his hands. She placed them on the floor and turned back towards him with large troubled eyes.

He gave her a quick urgent kiss.

They suddenly heard shouting from topside.

He whispered, "Don't come out until either Zan or I say it's okay for you. Lock this after I shut the door. And for your own sake, don't make a sound."

With that, the door shut in her face and Julie was plunged into complete darkness. She could hear Marc moving the clothes back to cover the saferoom's door. If she could hear those sounds so easily, then she knew she couldn't make a single sound if she wanted to survive this.

Julie quickly locked the inside of the door, preventing it from being opened from the closet area side. She spread out the blanket and pillow on the floor and felt in the bag for everything Marc had previously discovered.

The shouting from topside suddenly increased and Julie slapped her hand over her mouth to contain her startled cry.

The men's raised voices got louder as they approached the stairwell down to the suites and crew quarters. The sound of fists hitting flesh and accompanying grunts of pain were horrid noises. Julie's mouth went dry with fear. She tried to swallow, but her throat only made a solitary clicking sound. She had never before felt complete fear such as this. Her breathing was shallow, and she felt light-headed.

What if the men from the other boat hurt Zan or Marc? What if they took over the boat and sailed off with her hidden in the saferoom?

What would happen to her when they found her?

With the inevitable understanding of what that sickening situation would be, Julie started shivering and had to wrap her arms around herself to keep from making any noise.

Just then, several gunshots sounded.

Then quiet.

Then the boat's engines started up.

PAT ADEFF

Chapter Six

PIRATES? IN THE CARIBBEAN??

Julie wasn't sure how long she'd been in the saferoom. It could have been minutes. It could have been hours. Time had done an odd accordioning, played by her fears. She sat that way, breathing quietly with her hearing sense heightened to the point that she could hear her own heartbeat. This holding pattern lasted for what seemed forever.

Wouldn't Marc have come right back down to get her if they were safe?

What did it mean if no one came for her?

Would that mean that Zan and Marc were dead?

Please, God. Don't let that be it.

Except for the engine sound, the silence in the saferoom was louder than anything Julie had ever experienced. It was soul deafening. Her ears strained to pick up any noise at all above the rumble of the engines. After straining for sounds for too long, Julie drifted off unconscious in the aftermath of her fear.

She woke to the dark, no engine noise, and a soft ringing sound.

The phone in the bag!

On no! The noise will give her location away. She had to get her hands on the phone and stop its ringing.

She hurriedly fished around in the bag and found the offending phone.

She pushed the button to silence the ringing.

She just held it in her hand staring at the sudden light it offered to her dark prison.

"Julie?"

A thin voice came through to her.

"Julie?"

She pulled the phone to her ear. "He ... hello?"

Julie's shaky reply was met with a sigh of relief.

"Julie, you're safe. We're all safe. I'll be right down to let you out." Zan's voice never sounded sweeter.

She unlocked the door, waiting for someone to open it from the outside, since she couldn't seem to figure out how to do it.

Male footsteps pounded down the stairs and into Zan's room. Within just seconds, the saferoom door was flung open, and Julie launched herself into Zan's arms.

She clung to him while she released all her fear and terror in a wash of tears and sobs.

He just held her tight and let her emotional release happen, once again gently rubbing her back. The feel of her in his arms was exactly what he needed just then.

Zan could feel his trepidation and underlying dread slip away from him like a huge sigh.

They had made it. They were going to be okay.

"You're okay, kiddo!" Marc's voice came between them like a wedge as he ran into the room.

Zan's arms disappeared from around her and were replaced with Marc's arms. Not quite as nice as Zan's but also soothing, nonetheless.

Zan realized he had other duties to attend to and left the room quietly.

Marc watched him leave, a question in his mind about if he had read the situation correctly or not. Marc figured he'd just have to wait and see.

Eventually, Julie's crying reduced down to sniffles and the occasional hiccup and Marc released her.

She looked around and found a box of tissues on Zan's dresser. After blowing her nose and mopping up her tears, Julie was able to release a breath of relief.

"What happened?"

"First, you have to come up aft to see everyone. They want to see that you're okay for themselves." Marc took Julie's hand and gently drew her behind him up the stairs and lead her to the fishing deck on the back of the boat.

Julie glanced around, however, Zan was nowhere to be seen. Where had he disappeared to?

Then, Julie's face lit up when she saw the wide grins on the faces of Mr. VIP, Robert, and even Pierre. Other than the smiles, though, they looked like they'd been in a rowdy bar fight! Blooming bruises, bloody cuts, mussed hair, ripped clothes, and stances of victory were all worn like badges of honor.

Julie went over to each of them, giving them each a smile and hug. Mr. VIP almost crushed her ribs with his hug, lifting her off the floor while deafening her ear with his loud "Yee-haw!"

Even Pierre smiled and gave her a swift gentle squeeze.

"Wow! You all look ... just awful!" Julie's wide smile belied her words.

At that moment, Zan arrived back with the first aid kit under his arm and a gun in his left hand.

"Here you go, guys. Let's make sure none of your injuries gets infected." He tossed the kit to Pierre, who opened it for everyone's use, passing out antiseptic wipes, band aids, and antibiotic cream tubes.

"Marc?" Zan shifted the gun to his right hand. "Ready?"

"Yep, let's do it."

With slight puzzlement, Julie watched the two men leave.

Marc followed Zan to the foredeck, where they had their single prisoner secured with rope and duct tape. The man wasn't even struggling anymore. He just sat there with his head hung down in dejection, staring at the deck floor.

Zan had previously called in a *mayday* for help and the Turks and Caicos police and marine units were sending out a boat for the transport of their prisoner.

Unfortunately, the remaining members of the pirate boat had managed to escape with injuries similar to the ones decorating Zan's passengers. After Zan and the others fought off the attempted take-over, the others had fled, realizing it was not going to be an easy take like they had first expected it to be.

The one who had been in the water was unable to get back on board and floated in the ocean alone until Zan took pity on him and retrieved him from the water – after they had released the turtle first.

"So, anything you'd like to say?" Zan's voice was quiet yet firm.

The prisoner looked up sullenly, but then noticed the gun in Zan's hand. At that, his eyes shot up and his mouth dropped open.

"Don't worry. I'm not going to shoot you."

The prisoner relaxed slightly. Zan could see the mental machinations start regarding a possible escape.

"Yet."

The deadness in Zan's voice convinced him.

The prisoner slumped again, believing that Zan would do what he said.

Zan turned to Marc.

"We'll take turns watching him until the authorities arrive. They should be here within a couple of hours. I'll take the first watch. Come spell me in about 30 minutes, please."

"Will do." Marc headed back down to the fishing deck.

When he arrived, Pierre had already pulled out the good stuff, a bottle of Pappy Van Winkle's Family Reserve bourbon, and everyone was on the second pass-around. The laughter of relief had changed into the laughter of storytelling. Each man was explaining how he had fought off the pirates single-handedly. Guffaws and back-slapping accompanied each story.

Someone had found Julie a blanket when she started shivering with the aftershock of the event and had draped it around her. Marc moved over to her side and put a securing arm about her shoulders. Julie could feel his strength seep into her. It felt good as she leaned into his side.

Eventually, her shivers stopped, and she could breathe past the tight band that had been wrapped around her since the danger had started.

Looking around the small group, Julie felt a warmth in her heart for them all, even Mr. VIP. What was it about a dangerous situation that forged a group into being? This rag-tag group of individuals had somehow melded into a fighting group that had conquered over the bad guys. They had won the day and saved the girl – just like in a 1950's movie.

There wasn't anything more rewarding in anyone's life than something like that. It was the kind of day that everyone hoped that if it happened to them, they would live up to doing the right thing.

Listening to the boasting from the men, Julie realized that all she'd done was hide. Yet, at the same time, she also realized that she, as the lone female, would have suffered the greatest if all had been lost to the pirates.

Marc's arm tightened around her as though he was able to fathom her thoughts.

"It all worked out good. Don't second guess anything about it. You did the right thing."

Julie gave him a small wan smile in agreement. She knew in reality that she would have been more of a hindrance in the fight, especially against the pirates. However, that clashed with her personal belief that she was capable of doing anything she wanted to. In truth, there was no way she would have been able to fight off even one of those men by herself.

If she had happened to get out of their reach, there was nowhere to go to except into the ocean. And they could have easily pulled her out of the sea, or they could have prevented her from hanging onto the boat to catch her breath. In that case, she would have eventually tired after hours of treading water and possibly drowned.

It was hard for her to acknowledge the truth of this particular situation. It had all been so primitive and uncivilized, bringing up a fear in her that she'd never felt while living in New York. Julie had gotten used to a particular way of life in the city. What she had used to think of as possibly dangerous was nothing compared in ferocity to what she'd just survived.

However, survive is just what she'd done! She wanted to find out more about herself on this trip, and now she had. She knew that nothing that would happen in her life, from here on out, would be anything close to what she'd just been through. This realization made her feel a little bit tougher. A little bit wiser. A little bit freer.

And that thought brought a smile to her face. A real smile.

The others had surreptitiously watched her work through her thoughts and felt various levels of relief when that smile bloomed on her face just then. Their own smiles spread even wider.

Someone passed Julie that top-shelf bottle and she grinned her thanks right before taking a swig of the bourbon ... and then promptly started sputtering and coughing at the onslaught of the alcohol. She had just found out something else about herself; she wasn't a drinker.

She laughed along with the others while wondering where Zan had gone off to.

PAT ADEFF

Chapter Seven

THE CALM AFTER THE STORM

The authorities finally arrived and after almost no work at all had retrieved their prisoner. Zan and Marc answered every one of their questions to the best of their abilities. Luckily the TAC police had a good idea who the perpetrators were.

After questioning the lone remaining pirate, they had informed Zan that they even knew where the pirate boat's home port was probably located. They were sending out a detail at dawn to see if they could be captured.

They thanked Zan and the others for their dauntless displays of courage; thankful that the outcome had not been worse.

One of the marine officers informed Zan that the last boat that had fallen for their "turtle-caught-in-the-net" trick did not fare as well. They didn't go into detail, but everyone came to understand that lives had been lost, in very painful ways.

After Pierre put together a hastily gathered repast of cheese, crackers, chips, dip, and various sweets, each person had eventually made their way to their own cabin with full stomachs and calmed nerves.

Mr. VIP, himself, had crooked his arm and escorted Julie to the door of her cabin, making sure she locked it after shutting the door behind her. Julie smiled at his fatherly display of caring. Yep, even the most blustery person had a warm human side.

She took a hot shower, washing and conditioning her hair. After toweling it somewhat dry, she sat up in her bed with several pillows behind her and picked up her e-reader. However, none of the books caught her attention and she put it away.

She sat there in the middle of her bed, running over the events of the day in her mind. She was privately proud of the fact that she was able to admit to herself about the fear that she'd felt upon the realization that she was in grave danger.

What had been difficult to acknowledge before in her life, was now easy to confront.

Something had changed for her. Something profound.

With every devastating blow to her psyche over the past week, her soul had been cracked open wider and yet had repaired itself even stronger; like a muscle that had been torn and then became almost indestructible after being restored.

She liked it.

A lot!

And with that realization she knew that sleep was far away.

Julie got out of the bed and got dressed again.

Quietly opening her door, she checked to make sure she hadn't woken anyone else.

The boat had anchored again for the night, and the gentle swells of the ocean added a rhythm to her walking.

She ascended to what she now considered, "her spot" on the small deck just below the bridge area. The gentle breeze carried the scent of the ocean and surprisingly, a soft occasional whiff of flowers. Julie had no idea where the flowers could have come from, but she enjoyed the fragrance all the same.

Stretching out on the chaise lounge, she looked up at the vast array of stars in the sky. Without city lights to obscure their presence, Julie was in awe at just how many there were.

Some of them sparkled brighter; some were smaller; some created patterns that, Julie knew from her seventh-grade science class, had names, but she couldn't recall them.

Star gazing was rapidly becoming her favorite new hobby. She must have spent at least fifteen minutes just studying the various lights in the sky.

And unbeknownst to her, Zan had been up in the bridge, studying her with the same intensity she had for the nighttime sky.

He knew he should have made his presence known immediately, but had waited too long, and now it would be awkward for them both if he spoke.

So, he just stood there. Frozen to the spot.

He hadn't been able to decompress after that day's excitement. He'd almost lost his boat. More than that, he'd almost lost his passengers' lives. And Julie's.

When had she become so important to him?

She was not his usual type.

When he was around her, he was not himself. Instead of his usual ease with others, he'd become a surly, despicable man. Almost unapproachable. No wonder she was more interested in Marc.

Marc was friendly and cordial. He paid attention to Julie and took care of her.

All Zan had done was bark at her, with an occasional gentleness thrown into the mix, which threw off both of them.

How could he change that? Did he want to change that? She was only going to be around him for less than 24 more hours. As soon as they docked, she would walk out of his life.

Yet, he knew there was something special there between them. He could feel it.

Looking down at where she lay, he wondered if she felt it too.

Just at that moment, as though he'd spoken out loud, she sat up and turned her head towards the bridge.

Zan just stood there, feeling uncomfortable, as though he'd been caught staring at her ... which he was.

Julie had felt a presence behind her and knew before turning that it was Zan standing above her. When she turned and made eye contact, she could tell he felt a little bit like a deer in the headlights.

Before today, she would have been offended that she'd been being spied on.

Instead now, it didn't faze her at all. In fact, it became humorous to her way of thinking.

She smiled at him and stood up.

"Permission to approach." Julie added a salty salute to her address.

Zan's stricken expression lessened and he finally returned her smile.

"Permission granted."

He even managed a slight grin.

Julie climbed up the stairs and entered the bridge area.

As Zan's shoulders relaxed, he waved a hand, indicating that she should sit in one of the cockpit chairs.

She graciously nodded her head and sat down.

Zan plunked himself down in the other chair and they just sat there, making easy direct eye contact.

Finally, Zan stated, "I bet you never thought today's excitement was part of the cruise package you paid for."

Julie tilted her head slightly and gave him a wry half-smile.

"No. I must say that I didn't notice this on the reservation sheet anywhere."

They sat in companionable silence for a space and then Zan asked,

"Are you okay?"

Julie sat forward in her chair and clasped her hands together.

"I am!"

The look of slight surprise on her face made Zan laugh in relief. He had still been dodging stray thoughts of what might have happened to her, so the relief felt good. Julie joined him in the mirth and they finally ended their joyous session after several moments, wiping the tears of laughter from their eyes.

Zan reached out and gently took one of Julie's hands into his. He sat there rubbing the back of her soft hand, offering comfort, although he thought it was actually more for him than it was for Julie.

She seemed to have recovered from the whole incident faster than he had.

Another plus point to add to what he thought of her.

She definitely was someone special. In fact, he couldn't think of anyone else he knew who could have gone through what she'd been through this past week and come out the other end stronger.

In fact, she looked like she didn't have a care in the world at this moment.

Her calmness surrounded him like a warm caress, slowly evaporating any lingering fears he felt.

"Thank you."

It took Julie a moment to understand that Zan had just thanked HER!

"Zan. You saved my life today. Why are you thanking me?" Julie added a puzzled smile.

How do I tell her that her willingness to do what was needed, allowed me to focus on the others, knowing that she was safe? That it would have killed me if I had failed to safeguard her. That she's come to mean so much to me, and I don't even know how or why?

Unfortunately, Zan did not verbalize his inner thoughts very well this time.

"You follow orders very well." Even to his own ears, that didn't sound right. It didn't sound *right*? It sounded stupid.

"You're thanking me because I follow orders?" If Julie could have felt more confused or let down, she didn't know how.

Rising to her feet, Julie managed a small smile.

"Well, today was certainly an energy-draining day for me. And probably for you, too. Good night, Zan. I'll see you in the morning."

Zan was frozen in his seat and could barely mumble, "Good night, Julie..." as she left the bridge area and descended to her cabin. After she left, Zan just leaned forward, holding his head in his hands.

Julie was thankful no one else was up and about, since the tears were streaming down her face by the time she managed to get to her cabin and shut and lock the door behind her. Her weeping was silent. No outright sobbing, but the tears just wouldn't stop.

She slipped off her shoes and crawled under the covers, fully dressed. She buried her head in the pillow and just gave up.

She hadn't felt this bad even when Spencer had announced he couldn't marry her.

This pity-party went on for another ten minutes, and then the tears slowly dried up.

Julie just lay there quietly in the bed, coming back to herself bit by bit.

Finally, she realized she wasn't upset anymore. She had to check to see if she was just numb. Nope. Just not devastated anymore.

Well, that's a change. Hmmm.

Julie shrugged off the covers and sat up on the edge of the bed.

She didn't feel bad anymore! Usually if she was hurt, it would take days and days of worry, punctuated with frequently talking to one of her friends before the pain would fade.

Now, she'd just had a good cry and was almost all better.

It still troubled her that Zan obviously didn't feel the depth to their developing relationship that she had felt. Maybe she'd just misread him. It certainly wouldn't have been the first time she'd misread a man.

With a short sigh, she got up and changed into her pajamas for the second time that night. After brushing her teeth and washing her face, she finally felt ready for a little sleep.

When her head hit the pillow this time, there was only quiet.

She had the best night's sleep she'd had in several days.

Not so for Zan.

He knew he should try to get some sleep before the sun came up, but he couldn't bring himself to leave the bridge area. When he was here, he knew that he knew what to do.

He was an excellent ship's captain. He ran a successful charter fishing service. He had multiple repeat customers, which in and of itself was a testament to his professionalism.

He just wished he had that ability in talking to Julie.

Zan could have kicked himself for his verbal blunders. If he'd ever had a chance with her, he'd blown it completely this night.

All for the best, probably. She didn't live here in the islands. In fact, her home base was NYC! The two locations couldn't have been more different.

Yep. It was for the best.

And why didn't that thought make him feel better?

Maybe because he knew deep down that he was giving up. And it didn't feel good.

Chapter Eight

SAYING GOODBYE IS SUCH SWEET SORROW (APOLOGIES TO SHAKESPEARE)

When the boat finally motored up to the dock and was secured, Julie had her game plan at the ready. When she'd woken that morning, her head was clear.

She set herself the target to use the rest of the ex-honeymoon to figure out where she wanted the rest of her life to go.

It was energizing to actually be making her own plans for her future; not dimmed by others' intentions for where they thought she should go and what she should do.

Such as marrying Spencer. Julie knew deep down that her mother meant well and only wanted the best for her, which was why she'd been so delighted when Julie's boss had shown romantic interest in her.

Too bad, the best man for Julie hadn't been Spencer. Or the best friend, Charlotte. Julie wished them both lots of luck – sort of. Actually, she wasn't feeling THAT generous yet.

Honestly? She hoped that Spencer would eventually come to the realization that losing Julie was the biggest mistake he'd ever made. But, somehow, she knew that wasn't going to ever happen. Oh well. It felt good to create that satisfying scenario in her mind.

With a slight smile still on her face from that thought, Julie ascended to the main deck.

When Zan caught sight of her and the calm smile on her face, he knew that he'd truly blown it. He knew that if she had felt anything at all for him, she would have felt as stricken as he did. That was obviously not the case.

So, putting on his best captain's smile, he approached Julie.

"Except for the drama, how did you like your trip?"

Julie's smile dropped from her face. Was he speaking of their conversation from earlier?

Then she understood that he meant the pirate attack, and she was once again able to retrieve her smile.

"From a marketing point of view, you might want to add it to the itinerary. It was certainly exciting." Julie's voice sounded almost calm.

Zan was afraid that somehow he'd give away the secret fact that he'd held the pillow from the saferoom against his nose this morning, just so he could breathe in her sweet scent. He'd die of embarrassment if he thought anyone knew.

Giving a patented grin, he replied "I think I'll skip that. I don't imagine my insurance agent would appreciate the opportunity for error."

They stood there in weighted silence, just looking at each other. Each one wishing the other one would reach out somehow to mend the emotional rift that had come between them.

"Great sailing, Captain!" Mr. VIP's booming voice cut through the fog that had moved in between them somehow.

Zan turned away from Julie to accept VIP's hearty handshake.

"Never had a better time anywhere! I will be recommending this adventure to all my friends back home!" The cigar remained firmly wedged between the back teeth. "Especially the part where we fought off the pirates! You need to make that a staple!"

"Julie said the same thing!" Zan turned back to include Julie in the conversation, but she had already moved away and was speaking with Marc. With Marc who was standing too close to her in Zan's estimation. Way too close.

Julie could feel Zan's attention on her and Marc. She glanced over to see the scowl on his face just before he turned away.

"You know that he's interested in you, right?"

"What?" Julie had to ask Marc to repeat what he'd just said because her mind had wandered.

Marc smiled. "I said, you know that Zan is interested in you, right?"

Julie was at a loss for words. She just didn't know how to respond, so she didn't say anything.

Marc could see her discomfort and moved their conversation to safer waters.

"My boss is taking a couple of days to himself. Which leaves me with free time. Do you want any company?" Marc's accompanying smile was the smile of a good friend.

Julie thought it would be nice to have some company on a couple of her excursions. She was still scheduled for parasailing and horseback riding.

"Do you like horses?"

"Of course! I'm from Texas." Marc laughed.

"Well, that's great! Tomorrow is a ride and lunch. It should be fun!" Julie smiled back. "The best part is that it's already paid for."

"Oh, that's right. You mentioned something about an ex. Will you be all right with me being your one-plus?"

"It sounds perfect. We're doing this as friends, right?" Julie wanted to clarify Marc's intentions right up front.

This was something she would have never brought up before. And now she was very comfortable with her question.

Yep, she was making some definite good changes in her life. She gave herself a mental high-five.

Marc burst out laughing. "Jules, I sure wish you were interested in me, but I know that is not going to happen." He gave her a quick hug.

"That said, I'd love to be your friend and hang out together!"

A tenseness that Julie had been carrying in her neck and shoulders relaxed with Marc's statement to her. Now she had a friend on this foreign shore she could be with for a couple of days.

Her smile was brilliant and once again, Marc sure wished he was someone she was interested in.

Timing is everything.

And so Zan had caught the laugh and the hug and the brilliant smile from Julie towards Marc. If his spirits could have dropped any lower, they would have at that point.

Julie glanced back at the boat just after Zan had turned away to answer a question from Mr. VIP.

Marc noticed Julie's glance and her suppressed sigh. Grabbing both her bag and her tote along with his bag in one hand and her free hand in his other. "Come on, Jules! Let's get started."

Julie flashed Marc a thankful smile and started walking down the dock towards the car that was sitting there waiting for him.

Zan glanced over again and saw the apparent couple walking away, hands entwined. He also noted that Marc was carrying both their bags together. His thoughts and brow darkened at the same time and stayed that way for the next 48 hours.

Life on that boat was not particularly pleasant for either Pierre or Robert, who were sort of a captive audience to Zan's mood swings while they cleaned up from the sail.

One of the few good things that came out of those hours was that Robert learned how to follow orders and how to work faster. Surprisingly, he started feeling better about himself with every project that he completed.

By the second day, Zan actually came up long enough from his dark thoughts to breathe and noticed Robert's improved work ethic.

Interesting. Maybe he'd be able to give his older sister's kid back to her in a new and improved condition. That thought in and of itself brought his mood up a little bit more.

Pierre just kept his head down and did his usual thing, which was doing exactly what Zan wanted before Zan knew he wanted it done. It also helped that Pierre knew the foods that Zan preferred and was able to provide meals that satisfied.

It was only at night when Zan was up on the bridge looking at the stars that his thoughts became overwhelming to him. He felt like he didn't know himself anymore. And that was scary.

He didn't like that he'd fallen so hard in such a short time. That had never happened before and he just couldn't wrap his wits around why it had happened with Julie.

She wasn't anything special.

Yeah – right.
She wasn't that beautiful.
Liar.
She wasn't what he was looking for.
Oh? Then what was he looking for?
What WAS he looking for?

Chapter Nine

SAND AND SURF

When Marc walked into the hotel's lobby at 10:00 the next morning, he certainly looked comfortable and at home in his flip flops, shorts, and cotton shirt.

In fact, Julie realized that Marc looked good in everything he wore. She just wished she could be attracted to him as more than just a friend.

"Well! You look ready for the ocean ride." Julie's smile showed her approval as she stood up from the lounge chair she had just settled into moments before.

Marc's eyes gave her the once-over, taking in her own flip flops, shorts, and cotton blouse.

"I could say the same for you, too, Jules! You look great. But I gotta say that it feels weird not wearing boots for horseback riding."

"You can wear boots – if you want them ruined by the saltwater when we ride in the ocean." Julie laughed and grabbed her day-bag and followed Marc out to his rental car.

After verifying the directions for Marc, Julie sat back in the bucket seat of the convertible and enjoyed the Caribbean sunshine and fresh air.

Her hair was starting to flutter all over. She knew the tangles would be impossible to get out, so she pulled a hair tie out of her bag and secured the majority of it at the nape of her neck.

Then she leaned her head back on the soft leather headrest and closed her eyes. The gentle wind and sun felt wonderful.

Marc glanced over and saw the look of peace on Julie's face and was very glad she had asked him to accompany her to the horseback ride. He was starting to enjoy the oddity of having a just-friend of the opposite sex.

Usually, any relationship he had with a female was of the boyfriend/girlfriend type. Now, he could sort of relax and just enjoy their friendship.

It was certainly a new experience for him. And one he was starting to like. Although, he had to admit he was still attracted to Julie.

The drive to the starting point at the ranch took less than six minutes. They were supposed to ride in the Five Cays area. Julie had secured a private guide at one of the many riding stables.

After parking the car in the small dirt lot at the end of the driveway, Marc got out and came around to get Julie's door. Holding out his left hand, he helped Julie out of the front seat.

Julie felt like they were becoming good friends.

Marc shut the car door and started to say something to Julie when someone called out to them.

"Hello!" The friendly greeting came from a young man standing at the front of the stable, which sat at the far area of the dirt car lot. "Good! You made it!"

Marc and Julie both waved and walked over to the young man who was smiling at them.

"Mr. and Mrs. Prendergast – right?"

Julie paused in her step, realizing that she hadn't called the ranch to let them know the changes in the reservations.

"Um. No. Sorry about that." Julie tried to not stammer. "Uh, Spencer couldn't make it. I'm Julie and this is my ... friend, Marc."

The young man didn't miss a beat.

"Good to have you here, Miss Julie and Mr. Marc. Please follow me."

Julie and Marc shared a humorous raised-eyebrows look between themselves. Julie couldn't even imagine what the young man was thinking about her answer, if he was at all. Julie just shook her head at herself.

Just then, their guide turned around while walking so that he was walking backwards while facing them. "My name is Johnny."

"Yawny?" Marc wasn't sure if he'd heard correctly or not.

"Si! Johnny!"

So, for the rest of the day, both Julie and Marc called their guide Yawny. They didn't find out the spelling until much later, at which point they both rolled their eyes at their own misunderstanding.

Johnny had planned their day for them and told them their itinerary. They were to ride along the surf and in the ocean along Five Cays beach until they reached the southern tip of the beach, where they would enjoy a delicious meal at the Conch Beach Hut. All very low key and relaxed.

Johnny explained that his cousin was a cook at the renowned restaurant and that he'd have his own lunch in the kitchen while visiting. At the end of their meal, they would all ride back to the stable.

The Five Cays beach was going to be perfect for their horseback ride. The light blue ocean water was shallow enough that when they rode their horses in the water, the water would be coming up to their saddles.

That was the reason they were in shorts and flip flops.

The horses that Johnny chose for them were descendants of the original Paso Fino horses brought to the Caribbean from Spain. They were beautiful, gentle horses who seemed to look forward to the ride as much as Julie and Marc were.

Johnny's horse was one that he'd personally trained from its birth. Its name was King - and King was magnificent. He was eighteen years old with a mahogany hide and ebony mane and tail. He carried himself as though he knew just how wonderful he was.

Watching Johnny and his horse move together was an experience that even Marc, who was from Texas, had never seen before. The horse and rider were so in sync that they traveled as one.

Johnny did not use a saddle and at times even turned around and stretched out on King's back while telling them interesting bits of data about the islands.

King didn't miss a beat and accepted Johnny stretching out along his back as though the man was taking a nap.

Julie and Marc were both settled in saddles on their horses.

Julie's horse was a dappled gray named Morgano. He was fifteen years old and just as sweet-tempered as they come.

Marc's horse was an eight-year-old named Prince; and he was the direct offspring of King and looked almost as magnificent. Prince was a little bit more spirited due to his age, but nothing that Marc couldn't easily handle.

Their ride to the beach and then into the crystal waters was heavenly.

The sandy trail that lead from the stables to the shoreline was a gentle single-file stroll in powder white sand while hearing the soft sounds of birds singing in the short bushes that lined the trail.

Arriving at the end of the trail, the view of the ocean took Julie's breath away. The blue sky and jeweled-hued waters met at the far horizon.

The white clouds that moved across the sky were mesmerizing. The gentle breeze was cooling on her skin.

The horses seemed to know exactly what was expected of them. Without much guidance at all, they all ambled towards, and then into, the water. The clear water was the perfect temperature.

Julie was glad she'd brought a huge floppy straw hat that kept most of the sun off her face and shoulders.

She had slathered sunscreen over herself before Marc had come by the hotel to get her. She didn't want to get sunburned.

This particular sunscreen beauty routine was actually a habit ingrained in her by her mother. "*Too much sun and tanning of the skin will age you faster than anything else.*" Julie could hear her mom's voice in her head.

Stop it! Julie chided herself. *You're here for a reason, to find what you want from life. And that does not include bringing your mother along!*

Julie realized that her feet were now under the surface of the water and it felt wonderful! Something eased within her and a calmness seemed to envelope her entire being.

Marc laughed out loud at the wide smile that split Julie's face.

This ride was pure happiness.

Johnny had stopped speaking about the beauty of the Turks and Caicos Islands and was just enjoying the ride as much as the two of them were.

King went out a little deeper into the sea, but Julie was happy just to ride with the surface of the ocean level up to her thighs.

Marc hadn't missed the enticing view of the water on Julie's legs, but knew he was not going to make any comments. He was enjoying being in her company too much to jeopardize it by making her feel uncomfortable.

Their horses seemed to truly enjoy being in the water also. The ride was peaceful and brought a much-needed tranquility to Julie's life. For the first time in a long time, she was finally able to shut out her mental voices and thoughts.

She was just being – feeling the rhythm of the horse, hearing the soft shushing of the ocean on her legs, and enjoying the breeze caressing her body.

It felt decadent.

It felt needed.

It felt right.

Julie couldn't contain her laughter of pure joy. Throwing her head back with the feeling, her hat fell off her head. Luckily, her horse's back stopped it from falling into the water and Julie was able to retrieve it easily, giggling at it.

When Marc and Johnny joined her in laughter, it just felt perfect.

A little further down the beach, Johnny indicated with a wave of his hand that they should head towards the shore. In the distance, the Conch Beach Hut sign was just visible on shore.

Marc and Julie fell into line behind Johnny as he and King led the way to the shoreline just in front of the restaurant.

Johnny gathered the horses after Julie and Marc had dismounted and walked those magnificent beasts around to the back of the building where they could rest and have some water while the humans ate lunch.

Julie and Marc were shown to a table on the outside deck that faced the ocean under a shady sail-like canopy that allowed the breeze to flow over them while keeping the sun off them.

Immediately after being seated, two large fruity-type drinks were placed before them. Marc and Julie first stared at the drinks and then looked at each other for a moment.

Neither of them wanted a rum concoction this early in the day, no matter how beautiful the drinks looked.

The server noticed their hesitancy and asked, "Would you prefer these drinks without the alcohol?"

Julie and Marc both nodded in unison and then burst out laughing at their synchronization.

The server grinned and swept the drinks away. Within just a few minutes, new delicious-looking beverages were placed in front of them.

The scent of pineapple and coconut filled Julie's senses with the first sip of the drink. It was not only delicious, but refreshing, too!

Next came the fish tacos. The catch of the day was Mahi-Mahi fish. Nothing could have prepared them for the full flavor of the food. Maybe it was the gorgeous day. Maybe it was the horseback ride in the ocean. Maybe it was the great company.

But whatever it was, they both enjoyed it completely.

By the time they got to dessert, they were already full. But they just couldn't decline when the Bambara Rum Cake was brought to their table. There was no way they could turn down that particular edible delight.

A couple of elegant coffees rounded out their meal. Their perfect meal.

As they sat back in their chairs, feeling stuffed to the gills, the only thing they could possibly do was sit there and be completely contented. The ocean view. The call of the seagulls. The gentle breeze.

It almost made Julie sleepy. Almost, but not quite.

This was the feeling that she had been looking for in her life. This feeling of contentment and happiness.

She wished there was some way to put this into a bottle to take home with her somehow.

She knew that in the days to come that she would need to be able to recall this exact moment. The memory of it should help her handle everything that she needed to confront.

"Hey. What happened to the peaceful look that was on your face a moment ago?" Marc's soft voice broke through her musings.

"Oh. Reality. You know." Julie tried to not sound too down, especially after how great the day had been so far.

She shifted in her chair and put a smile back on her face. "However, all that can wait for later."

"What happens later?"

Marc's look of friendly concern just pierced through Julie's defenses and she told him everything that had happened over the past couple of years.

The server brought more coffee, and Julie continued to tell Marc about working in New York and falling in love with her boss, and being stood up at the church, and her best friend's betrayal.

Marc's occasional "and then what happened," or "hm-mm?" comments gently urged Julie to tell him the complete story.

When she'd finished, she just sat there, staring out over the ocean. Marc was a great listener and it felt right to have told him everything.

So, they both sat there in companionable silence for a few minutes.

About the time that Julie felt she should ask Marc about his life, Johnny showed up at their table with his huge grin. "It's time to head back to the stables. How was your lunch?"

Marc's smile said it all. "It was beyond great! This was excellent."

"Good! I like my clients to be happy!"

Julie and Marc stood up and followed Johnny to the edge of the beach in front of the restaurant where he'd already tied the horses.

They mounted up and headed back out into the ocean. The pace was slower moving up the beach's shoreline and they all enjoyed the rest of the ride back to the stables.

Marc's rental car slowly pulled up to the front of Julie's hotel.

They were both slightly sunburned – in spite of Julie's sunscreen ritual – and relaxed and happy.

The day had turned out to be a great time for both of them. As well as for Johnny when he received his large tip from Marc.

Julie was happy to see that Marc wasn't a tightwad with his money and had rewarded him with a smile of acknowledgement for his generosity.

Sitting in the car, neither of them wanted the day to end yet. It was almost dinner time and it was just a natural comment for Marc to say, "Pick you up in an hour for dinner?"

Julie smiled and said, "That sounds great! See you then."

The doorman stepped over and opened Julie's door for her. She swept out of the car, turned back and smiled at Marc.

Then, with her day bag in one hand, she gave a little wave and disappeared through the hotel's front doors.

Marc didn't waste any time in heading to his hotel for a quick shower and change of clothes.

Julie took a little longer with her shower and shampooed her hair. Whatever the tropical coconut concoction was in the shampoo dispenser located on the wall in the shower, it was wonderful, and it made her hair soft and luxurious.

Exactly one hour later, Julie exited her hotel's front doors and walked over to Marc's car, which had just pulled up.

Marc gave a low whistle of admiration to Julie's transformation. Not that he thought she looked anything less than lovely earlier that day. But tonight, she was a complete knockout.

Her sun-kissed skin was not covered with make-up. And the soft peach glow on her face made her eyes stand out. Her hair looked alluring and its soft scent on the breeze smelled even better. When she slid into the front seat, her short floral dress tugged up enough for him to see the soft inside of her thigh.

Whoa! Stop! Marc rapidly corralled his thoughts. He knew with absolutely certainty that Julie would back away from their friendship if he showed any signs of male to female attraction.

So, he quickly ended the whistle and added with a cocky grin, "You sure do clean up good, Miss Julie."

"Thank you, Marc. And I accept your compliment in the spirit it was intended – good friends. You clean up pretty good yourself."

They both relaxed and laughed.

"So, where are we going?" Julie was looking forward to a great dinner. She had worked up quite an appetite on the horseback ride, in spite of the huge lunch.

"There's a great restaurant called the Coconut Bistro. They offer everything from your standard Surf 'n Turf to shrimp and avocado spring rolls to an herb-crusted roast lamb rack. Also, they're renowned for their international wine list. I think you'll love it."

"Sounds perfect!" Julie beamed, and then added, "You sound like you know the place."

"Nope. Just read the online menu." Marc grinned and put on some music; their ride to the restaurant was thoroughly enjoyable.

Both Julie and Marc were leaning back in their chairs, fully satiated from the second excellent meal they had enjoyed that day.

"I don't think I'll be able to get up and walk!" Julie placed her hand over her stomach and smiled.

"Luckily, we don't need to move just yet." Marc felt the same way. He was basking in the wonderful company, easy conversation, and robust fare.

The wine he'd ordered to go with their dinner was excellent and he was enjoying the last smooth sip from his glass.

As he placed his glass back on the table, he noticed that Julie's glass was still half full.

"Wasn't the wine to your liking?" His brows pulled up in question.

"What? No. It was great." Julie shot him a smile. "I just don't drink much anymore."

She was still remembering the day of her almost-wedding and the amount of spirits she had consumed. Nope, no more overindulging for her.

Sure, it worked at the moment to help calm her down, but in the long run it hadn't helped at all. It had just postponed confronting the reality of the situation.

"So, what's on the agenda for tomorrow? I have one more day of freedom before I have to report back to my boss."

Marc's demeanor showed Julie that he actually liked his work, which puzzled her completely. She had found Mr. VIP to be overbearing and hard-to-take for the most part.

"Parasailing! Have you ever been before?"

"Nope, not at all. And I have to reluctantly admit that I am slightly cringing when it comes to thinking about the heights we'll be at." Marc's chagrined smile was almost boyish.

"I'm sorry! I had no idea. We can skip it if you want." Julie didn't want to put anyone through something they weren't comfortable doing.

"No! Actually, I think I'd like to confront that particular fear of mine. I know, analytically that it's safe and that I won't crash or anything. I'm hoping that I'll love it and this will be the end of my dislike of heights.

"Besides," Marc grinned. "If you're my audience I might not scream and cry like a little kid."

Julie's laugh joined his and they both sat there chuckling at the picture Marc had created. Slowly, their laughter died away and they just sat here in companionable silence.

Julie thought she was very lucky to have met Marc on this trip that could have turned out totally awful.

And just as quickly, her thoughts went to Zan. She wished she knew what had happened there. She thought they had started a ... what?

What was it she thought she'd had with Zan? She knew she was attracted to him. She thought he was attracted to her, a least when he wasn't barking at her.

"Where did you go?" Marc's soft question pulled Julie from her musings and she realized that she'd been sitting there staring at the tablecloth for some time.

"Let me guess. Zan?" Marc's question was asked with a soft understanding shaded with an undercurrent of resignation.

Julie reached over and covered Marc's hand with her own.

"Marc, I'm sorry. I don't know why he even entered my mind." Julie tried to give her answer with an upbeat nonchalance.

However, Marc wasn't buying it.

"Jules, you don't ever have to hide what's going on when you're with me. We're friends, remember?"

Julie patted the back of his hand and sighed. She gave Marc a small smile of apology.

"You're right. Friends. In fact, right now you're my best friend in the whole world."

The thought made Marc grin.

"The whole world?"

"Yep. Especially since my last best friend took off with my fiancé, who was by-the-way, also my boss, so I guess I'll be looking for a new job."

It surprised Julie that she wasn't more upset at that prospect.

"Okay. I know you're a photographer. What kind?"

"All kinds, but mostly marketing pix. Whatever the client needs, I provide."

"Hmmm." Marc looked thoughtful for a moment.

"You know. It's possible my boss might know somewhere that needs a photographer. In fact, he's meeting today and again tomorrow with the Island Chamber of Commerce on a business deal. Would you like me to check?"

Julie had never considered that knowing Mr. VIP might turn out to be a helpful connection for her.

"Wow! If it's not any trouble, I would love that!" Julie decided that her luck might have taken a turn for the better. "Will your boss be okay doing that?"

"Actually, he's a lot more human than he puts on. He frequently has me doing small anonymous favors for people who need help. It's kind of his secret. He thinks that most people look at him as a slightly pompous character."

"Slightly?" Julie's eyebrows raised up in humor.

"Well ... I guess it depends on the person." Marc's grin matched Julie's.

The rest of the evening went smoothly for Julie and Marc's newfound friendship.

After dropping her off at her hotel, Marc called his boss and made the request.

He'd just have to wait to see if he could help Julie or not. He hoped he could.

"Okay! I give. Why do you have a cat-who-ate-the-canary look on your face?"

Julie had just gotten into Marc's car so they could head out for their parasailing adventure.

Marc just kept smiling but finally issued an "Ouch!" when Julie play-punched him in his arm.

While grinning from ear to ear, Marc put the car into drive, and they moved out into the sun from under the porte-cochere of the hotel.

"Tell me!" Julie threw her head back and laughed.

It was a moment that took Marc's breath away. Her zest for life that morning was contagious and Marc joined the laughter.

"I've got good news for you!"

Then he didn't say anything; just smiled.

"Tell me!" Julie couldn't contain the good feeling she had since she'd woken up that morning. She just knew that everything was going to work out just fine.

"My boss spoke with his business friend at the island's chamber of commerce. They are in the process of putting together a new marketing campaign for next season and they are in need of a professional photographer. When he told them about you, they asked him if he might be able to talk you into taking the job for them."

Julie was thunderstruck into silence. But just for a minute.

"A job? Here?" Julie was still trying to process what Marc had said.

"Yep. It's yours if you want it."

"Wow."

And that seemed to be all that Julie could say for the next five minutes of driving.

She looked around at the island and saw the beauty of it all as though she was already setting up her camera.

Marc glanced over occasionally just to watch the various expressions move across Julie's face.

He finally buried a sigh and asked, "So, what do you think?"

"Wow."

"Yes, you said that before."

"Thank you?" Julie's soft smile melted Marc's heart completely. He reached over and softly grasped her hand in his.

Then in a move that surprised them both, he lifted her hand to his lips and gave a gentle kiss.

Chapter Ten

ANYTHING I CAN DO, SHE CAN DO BETTER

"Alexander! You're just not listening to me! You are not hearing a word I'm saying!"

By the end of the sentence, Zan's father was almost shouting, which was not unheard of.

Mr. DeKeurge's secretary, Ana, was sitting at her desk in the outer office, trying valiantly to ignore the conversation she could easily hear coming through the heavy carved oak door that led into the CEO's office.

Her main concern was that someone would walk into her area and then hear the argument that had been taking place over the past few minutes.

Just to ensure privacy, Ana got up and walked over to the other door that led into the outer hallway. She opened that door, put up the Do Not Disturb sign, and then locked the door from the inside.

She crossed back over to her desk, took a seat, and plugged in her earbuds, playing some music. She knew that her boss would appreciate her muting of their conversation, and she knew that he also wouldn't want her desk abandoned right now.

It was a fine line, but Ana had worked for the DeKeurge family for over 20 years and knew her way around.

Inside the CEO's office was a different story. Zan didn't feel like he knew his way around his father at all right now.

They had had this difficult conversation more and more frequently. Mr. DeKeurge wanted Zan to step up and take over the reins of the company.

Zan had no intention of doing that. He knew he wasn't built for running the company, dedicating his entire life for the next 40 years.

Besides, he had different ambitions for himself. He wanted to build his own charter fishing company, with a fleet of top-of-the-line boats, covering the Caribbean.

He wanted to build something of his own.

The DeKeurge Foundation was generations old, historically passed down to the next eldest son. The fact that Zan's father loved his work made it very hard for Zan to get him to understand his reticence on taking over the company.

The truth was that Zan's younger sister, Jaimee, was the perfect CEO for the family foundation. In fact, she lived and breathed it.

Jaimee's work hours were astounding. Her ability for knowing what the Foundation needed to do next was spot on. And her passion for it was staggering.

The only problem was that she wasn't the eldest son.

Zan knew his father would understand and agree if he could just get him past the generational tradition thing.

"Dad." Zan kept his voice even so that the conversation wouldn't devolve into the usual fight, which never accomplished anything productive.

"I am listening to everything you're saying. I am." Zan paused there to see if it would sink in that he was actually listening.

Mr. DeKeurge was about to continue with his rapidly escalating tirade but stopped.

He closed his mouth and just looked at Zan while taking some breaths.

Zan looked back at his father, hoping he was getting through. He knew how much this meant to his dad, but he also knew that he had to go for what he wanted in his life.

He truly wished that it was the family business, but Zan knew that would never fulfill him.

He also knew that the family business would thrive more than it ever had under the leadership of his little sister.

Now if he could just get the senior DeKeurge to see that also.

"What can I say to change your mind, Son?" Mr. DeKeurge looked like he would give anything to get Zan to agree to his wishes.

Zan took a deep breath. He knew that his future, his family's future, and the family Foundation depended on what happened here and now.

He got up and walked over to the polished wood credenza where the coffee service was already set up.

He hoped he could buy some thinking time by getting himself a cup of coffee.

After he poured himself a cup, he turned to his father and, gesturing to the coffee pot, asked without words if he wanted a cup, too.

Mr. DeKeurge hesitated a moment, but then nodded "yes."

Zan poured a second cup and carried it over, setting it down on the desk in front of his dad.

He then returned to his place on the leather couch and set his cup on the glass coffee table which was centered in front of the couch with two matching leather armchairs on either end.

Zan took a sip and watched while his father did also. It was apparent that neither of them wanted to actually be angry with the other.

Their bond of father and son had always been strong. It was only their vision for the future of the company where they didn't see eye to eye.

Zan leaned back in the couch, sipping his coffee, trying to look nonchalant as well as gauge the waters he was currently attempting to navigate.

As long as both he and his father kept their tempers in check, this might turn out to be a profitable conversation for both of them.

Zan could only hope.

"Dad. I would like to make a business proposition to you. I would like to have your agreement that you will just listen. Don't judge it before I've finished the presentation, however much you might want to.

"Basically, I'm requesting that you listen to what I want to offer as though you've never heard any of it before. I believe that what I'm going to propose will benefit everyone involved, as well as securing the future of the Foundation." Zan then paused.

"And yes, the future of the Foundation is very important to me, also."

Zan knew that if he could get his father to actually listen, there might be a chance they could come to an agreement where everyone could win, and the family wouldn't be torn apart.

So, he just sat on the couch, waiting patiently for his father to make up his mind about listening.

Time seemed to stand still.

Finally, something passed between father and son that calmed them both. A trust. A family love that stretched back generations that couldn't be broken.

Mr. DeKeurge settled back in his chair and took several sips of his coffee before speaking.

"Alexan..." He paused for a breath. "Zan. I will listen to your presentation. I will try to keep my thoughts to myself, and I will try to understand everything you are going to show me. More than that, I can't promise anything."

Zan felt himself slowly relaxing. He knew that if his father was willing to actually listen and look at the presentation instead of assuming he knew what Zan was going to say, Zan knew they would eventually come to an agreement which worked for everyone.

And with that hopeful outlook, Zan launched into the presentation.

Half an hour later, Zan finished up and Mr. DeKeurge sat at his desk in deep thought. Zan knew he was considering everything that Zan had stated.

They must have sat there in silent stillness for at least two minutes, which felt like an hour.

Each consumed by his own thoughts.

Zan sat calmly on the couch, waiting for whatever his father would say next.

He was surprised when his dad leaned forward and hit the intercom button for Ana.

"Ana. Could you please have Jaimee come to my office. And please see that we have fresh coffee and some sandwiches."

"Yes, Mr. DeKeurge. Immediately."

Zan's father then sat back in his chair, silently, still thinking. He did not meet Zan's eyes while he contemplated the presentation information.

In spite of his nerves, Zan just sat quietly on the couch, waiting to see what would occur.

"You'll excuse me for a moment." Mr. DeKeurge got up and went into his private bathroom.

After the door closed behind him, Zan let out a breath that he was unaware of having held. He also shook out his hands because they suddenly felt a little numb.

Out in the reception area, Ana was just getting back to her desk from the small kitchen located in the CEO's suite.

She had earlier brewed a fresh pot of coffee and had it ready to pour from an insulated carafe.

The sandwiches had been sent up from the deli early that afternoon, and all she had to do was unwrap them and place them on a plate.

Same with a few cookies from the bakery she had picked up on the way into work that morning. The tray she was carrying looked inviting.

Ana heard the knock at the door. She had forgotten that she had locked the door earlier.

She set the tray on the corner of her desk and crossed to the door, unlocking it swiftly.

Jaimee was standing there, looking rested and well dressed as usual.

"Hi, Ana. Dad called for me?" Jaimee walked into the office.

Ana closed the door behind her and once again locked it.

Jaimee raised an eyebrow in question.

"Mr. DeKeurge and Alexander have been in conference for the past hour. I was just taking them some fresh coffee and a bite to eat."

"Here, Ana. I'll just take the tray in with me." Before Ana could protest, Jaimee picked it up and crossed to the heavy wood door leading into her father's office.

Easily balancing the tray on one hand, Jaimee opened the door with the other like a seasoned food server.

Ana was so proud of the woman Jaimee had become. She understood completely the passion that Jaimee had for the Foundation.

Ana was praying that Mr. DeKeurge had actually listened to Zan this time. She had been witness to more than one argument between the father and his two children, and although she had definite opinions about what would be the best choice for the next CEO, she could only watch and wait.

Mr. DeKeurge had just settled back into his chair when Jaimee came through the door carrying the tray of refreshments.

Zan jumped up to help his sister. She smiled her thanks as he took the tray from her and placed it on the side credenza. Jaimee automatically served a sandwich and fresh coffee to her father.

She was a bit unnerved by his steady gaze as she placed the plate and cup and saucer in front of him.

She smiled a small smile at him as she removed the cup and saucer he'd used earlier.

Zan watched the interchange between them from his place on the couch.

Hiding a small smile behind a sip of the fresh coffee, he felt that maybe this time it might work.

He sure hoped so.

"Jaimee." Their father's voice didn't give any indication of what he was thinking. It was just a businesslike tone.

"Yeah, Dad." Jaimee just stood there at the credenza, waiting for what he was going to say.

"That is the last time you will serve me coffee as though you were my assistant."

Both Zan and Jaimee held their breaths, wondering where this was going.

Jaimee knew that Zan had planned on having another talk with their father that afternoon. She knew that Zan truly did not want the mantle of responsibility for the Foundation.

He had shared with her his plans for his charter business. She'd even helped him write up his business plan.

But none of that would matter if their father was not in agreement with them.

"Please have a seat." Mr. DeKeurge indicated one of the chairs in front of his desk.

Then, looking over at Zan, he indicated for Zan to take a seat in the other chair.

After both his children were situated in front of him, he sat back and his face relaxed into a gentle smile.

"Alexander, your presentation was well thought out and spoke of the intelligence and diligence you put forward in creating it."

Zan nodded once, waiting for his father's final decision.

Jaimee sat as still as she could.

"You both know my viewpoint on who I thought should take over for me with the Foundation." Mr. DeKeurge waited for them to both nod their understanding of his statement.

And neither of them missed that he had used the word "thought" instead of "think."

He paused for a moment and then stated, "Jaimee, I have done you a great disservice. Alexander has helped me see what needs to occur for the best outcome for our Foundation."

A small smile broke the seriousness of his words. "And also, for both Zan and you of course."

Zan and Jaimee were still not able to relax completely. Their father had not yet stated outright a change in his viewpoint.

"It is my decision that you, Jaimee, should take over as CEO."

There it was! The answer Zan and Jaimee were waiting for.

"And you, Alexander, have my complete agreement and backing for your charter business ... on one condition."

"Yes, Sir?" Zan was surprised his dry throat could even croak out the words.

"I would like you to continue, with Jaimee's agreement of course, attending the social functions when we donate money to our charities."

Zan couldn't believe the change in his father's viewpoint. It appeared that he had finally gotten through.

He wondered what the change had been and why it had happened.

He was ruminating over the change when he felt his sister's foot kick him from where she was sitting next to him.

That brought him back to the present very rapidly.

"Of course!" Zan didn't have to think twice about agreeing to his father's request.

In fact, showing up at the social engagements were the only part of the Foundation work that he enjoyed.

"That is," Mr. DeKeurge added while looking at Jaimee, "if Jaimee wants you to do that."

Jaimee didn't hesitate at all. "Of course! That takes me off the hook of having to take the time for the presentation and pictures. I'd rather be meeting and greeting the guests."

Jaimee's open smile said it all.

"Father, would you also consider making time for attending the events still?"

Mr. DeKeurge gave a wry smile.

"You'll have to check with your mother about that. I believe she has already made daily plans for what I will be doing for at least the next twenty-four months, if not longer."

The three of them sat there smiling contentedly at each other.

Out in the outer office, Ana sat in anticipation of the outcome. Just then, the intercom came to life.

"Ana, could you please come in."

Ana grinned at hearing Jaimee's voice on the intercom for the first time. Good things were happening.

Chapter Eleven

HOME SWEET HOME

When the long flight from the Turks and Caicos Islands finally touched down at LaGuardia Airport in NYC, Julie felt as confused as when she had left the island.

The flight had seemed even longer than usual. Nothing had kept her interest for more than a few minutes. She couldn't even sleep.

She felt keyed up in a weird sort of way; excited about her future and frightened about her future and in despair about her future.

None of it made sense to Julie, but she knew she had to try to get her head on straight if she was going to make any headway with her folks.

She wasn't as concerned about her dad as she was about her mom. Julie's mom had always had certain standards that she assumed Julie would meet. It wasn't as though Julie and her mom fought.

It was just that her mom was a force not many people could withstand, including Julie.

Over the years, through high school and college, Julie had just found it easier to go along with her mom's wishes.

It was obvious that she had Julie's best interests at heart when it came to decisions, such as what kind of profession to aspire to, which boys to date in high school, how to dress, how to behave, basically how to live one's life correctly.

Julie suspected that most of her mom's ideas had been ingrained into her by her Connecticut upbringing.

Just how she was going to explain that what she needed to do for herself, first depended on her own understanding of it.

Some of her ideas were still murky, and Julie knew that she needed some time to fully decompress a little.

Julie hoped her mom would understand and let her be for a week or so without trying to fix whatever she decided her daughter needed to fix.

Thanks to Marc, she now had a new job that sounded wonderful. However, that job was not in the continental USA. In fact, it wasn't even an American territory.

Maybe she'd learn a new language – or not. The citizens of The Turks and Caicos Islands spoke great English. But she knew that she'd want to know the local dialect, sort of an English based Creole.

It was locally referred to as Turks and Caicos Creole and was similar to other Caribbean Creole languages.

Its blending of English vocabulary with African grammar made for a beautifully lyrical sound.

Focus, Julie!

She knew she only had a few hours before arriving at her parent's home, located on the Long Island Sound in Guilford, Connecticut.

Julie's mom was a direct descent of family who had lived there, dating back to the Revolutionary War.

The family name - her mom's maiden name - was on many of the signs of the local businesses.

Growing up, Julie hadn't actually thought about it much. She knew they were well off, but she hadn't made the historical connection until one particular 5th grade lesson on local history.

When she kept hearing her mom's family name mentioned by the teacher, it finally hit her why most of the kids didn't invite her to their birthday parties.

She wasn't considered one of them. She was somehow special.

Sure, she'd had a close group of weekend friends whose moms were also good friends with her mom. They all belonged to the local yacht club.

It had just never occurred to Julie that a day trip into New York City wasn't something that everyone did when they needed to purchase their new wardrobes for the next school year.

Now, she intended to completely upend her parents' plans for her life.

First of all, she wasn't using her very expensive Harvard degree in sociology to earn a tony position with some renown educational group, which would have been the *correct* career for her.

With a wry smile, Julie realized she'd probably actually use that degree more on The Turks and Caicos Islands than she ever had before.

She also realized that her parents expected her to marry well; not some captain of a fishing boat.

Wait! Where had that thought come from?

Julie shook her head and tried to bury Zan from her thoughts. Granted, it was a particularly difficult task, but she had to keep trying.

After all, there couldn't be a future for them. Zan had made it pretty clear that he wasn't interested in her.

Besides, Julie knew that her interest in him was just some sort of rebound reaction.

Any normal gal would have responded to any male's interest after being dumped at the altar – right?

Okay.

Then why wasn't she attracted to Marc that way?

And why did Zan keep sneaking into her thoughts?

Maybe because there HAD been a connection between them? A real connection?

Wait!! Stop it. Just stop it.

Easier said than done.

When Julie's rental car finally turned into her parents' drive, she'd figured it all out – sort of.

First, she was going to beg exhaustion to stall any questions. Then she hoped that by morning some brilliantly worded plan would come to mind; hopefully before she went down to the kitchen for coffee.

The huge front door opened before Julie even got out of the driver's seat.

Both her parents came out, moved swiftly down the steps and around to her door.

Her dad had it opened and had wrapped his arms around Julie before she realized that this was exactly what she needed.

Next, her mom gave her a very hard hug and wouldn't let go. Julie finally laughed when her dad gently put his arms around both of his ladies.

They stood that way for some time. No words. Just unconditional love.

Finally, her mom released her death grip hold and took Julie's hand instead, leading her into the house.

Julie could have sworn she saw tears in her mom's eyes.

Her dad grabbed her bags out of the back seat and following the women into the house, left the luggage next to the front door.

Julie and her folks landed in the back parlor room of the house.

This was the room that had always seemed to Julie like what a home should be.

No guests were ever allowed in this room, so Julie's mom was very willing to have it remain comfortably cluttered and not looking like something from *Homes and Gardens* magazine.

Julie's mom pulled her over to one of the wonderfully overstuffed couches and still holding her hand sat down. Julie sat down next to her.

It was scaring Julie a little bit.

Her mom, who was usually coiffed and polished, looked a little bit bedraggled.

In fact, Julie knew something was off because her mother was not wearing lipstick; not even a lip balm.

She couldn't remember the last time she'd ever seen that.

Her dad looked fine. He seemed slightly reserved, but other than that he seemed okay.

It was her mother who appeared agitated and not fully in control.

"Mom?" Julie squeezed her mom's hand.

"Yes, Dear?" Her mom's eyes looked a little dazed.

"Mom? Are you all right?"

"Hmmm?"

Julie shifted her gaze to her dad to get his reaction. All he did was give her a slight smile.

"Okay. Now you're scaring me. What's going on?"

Julie's mom glanced at her husband before taking in a deep breath. Then she slowly let out the breath and spoke.

"Julie, your father and I have had a few, um, conversations while you were gone. With his... help, I've come to some new understandings."

Then she just sat there, silently staring at the floor, still holding Julie's hand, unconsciously running her thumb over the back of it.

Once again Julie looked over at her dad who just shrugged back at her with another slight smile.

After several more moments of stilted silence, Julie finally blurted out "Is someone dying?"

"What?!" Julie's question seemed to have startled her mother out of whatever mood she was in the middle of.

"Good heavens! Why would you say something like that?"

Julie was glad to see the usual light come back into her mom's eyes while at the same time her spine straightening up.

"Maybe because you are acting really weird?" Julie couldn't contain the half smile forming on her lips.

At that, her mother's eyes narrowed a bit and she looked straight at Julie like she had done so many times in the past.

"Young lady, that smart mouth of yours is not a credit to our family."

Julie relaxed. Her mom was back.

However, just then, her dad cleared his throat in a definite manner towards her mom.

Julie's mom glared over at her husband for a few moments. When he didn't back down, she finally shrugged her shoulders, sighed, and turned back to Julie.

"Dear, there is something I need to say to you."

"Can this possibly wait until tomorrow? It was a very long flight and I'm really tired."

"I wish it could, but it can't."

Julie's mom seemed to deflate a little bit. "If I don't get this said now, I don't think I ever will be able to say it again."

Julie stifled a sigh and gave her mom what she was hoped was an encouraging smile, silently willing this conversation to be over soon.

"Apparently, your father thinks..."

Julie's father once again cleared his throat, this time in a semi-threatening manner.

Just how did he manage to articulate whole sentences with just a sound? Julie thought she might like to have that skill someday.

"... as do I ..." Julie's mom slowly added to her previous statement before continuing, "that apparently the things I thought were in your best interest in the past might not have been so."

There were a few moments of silence and then her father cleared his throat once again, but this time the sound indicated *please continue.*

Yep, that was sure some skill.

"AND..." Julie's mom lifted an eyebrow back at her husband which spoke volumes.

Julie wondered why she'd never noticed before that her parents had their own language.

"... I have decided that you should live your life the way you see fit. Even if I disagree with some choices you might make, it is your life and you should live it without my guidance."

She then quickly added, "No matter how correct my suggestions are." And sat back on the couch, obviously finished with her speech.

Julie sat there in stunned silence not knowing how to respond.

She'd just spent the better part of the long flight home trying to come up with a plan to get her mom to back out of her life a little bit, and now she'd just been handed her wish on a silver platter – albeit disgruntledly so.

"Julie?" Her dad's gentle voice intruded into her thoughts and brought her back to the present.

"Um. I'm not sure what to say." Julie turned to her mom. "Thank you for what you said. I know that must have been hard for you."

Julie's mom just rolled her eyes in response.

Julie's dad just chuckled.

All Julie could think was *well the next few weeks should be interesting!*

Chapter Twelve

THE BIG APPLE

Julie took the time over the next week to put order into her plans. She didn't have to return to the islands for her new job for another ten days and she intended to use those days to bring her previous life in NYC to a satisfactory close.

Surprisingly, her mother had actually been very helpful with some of her suggestions, after Julie had reluctantly asked for her advice.

At first, Julie had a little back-off asking for her mom's opinion, as did her mother, wondering if she should give advice or not. But after a few halting moments, they worked out a new way to converse.

Julie actually felt as though her mom and she might be rising to a new level in their relationship. It was new and needed some work still, but it brought both of the women a glimmer of hope.

Also, surprisingly, Julie had received two vaguely worded text messages, one from Spencer and another one from Charlotte.

It seemed they both wanted to speak with her. Yeah, right. Don't think so. Julie easily deleted the messages.

She even thought of blocking their numbers but decided she might still need them at some future time for, well, whatever. It wasn't like their numbers were taking up valuable space in her phone.

First, she called Sarah, one of her co-workers at her soon-to-be-not-employed-at place of work. Sarah seemed to be truly happy to hear from her and commiserated over the disastrous wedding failure.

It seemed that most of the office had heard about it, surprisingly from Charlotte who had contacted a couple of Julie's co-workers who were mutual friends.

Sarah mentioned that no one at work had seen much of Spencer, except for his arrivals and departures from the office, first thing in the morning and last thing at night.

After Sarah transferred Julie to Human Resources, a day and time were set for Julie to come into the office later that week and gather her personal items.

The HR Director let it slip that a "very nice severance check" had been left for Julie to pick up when she was there. The money wasn't a complete surprise for Julie, but she was glad for the gesture, nonetheless.

So, Julie decided that the next day was when she would go to her apartment in the city and box most of her stuff up.

Her parents had said she could store it all at their home, while she was contracted to work at the Turks and Caicos Islands.

She called an associate of hers whose husband owned a moving company and scheduled for a couple of the moving guys to meet her at the apartment at 8:00 in the morning.

She also arranged for them to bring boxes, tape, padding, and everything else that would be needed for the packing.

She was surprised at how calm her life had become in spite of all the changes happening.

Or maybe, it was just the fact that something in her had changed and she had become calmer, no matter what was going on around her.

Her scheduled meeting with Spencer had been nonexistent.

Apparently, he had fled the office already.

His assistant apologized to Julie, something about an unexpected meeting. When asked if she wanted to reschedule their meeting, Julie just replied no.

Slightly bemused, Julie went back to her office.

She was boxing up the last of her personal items when she heard a knock on her door.

Looking up, she expected to see another one of her workmates. All morning, there had been a steady stream of friends stopping by, wishing her all the best with her new job.

Yep, word had spread quickly.

Instead, it was Charlotte standing there.

Julie debated on giving her the cold shoulder but realized that wouldn't be in the best interest of anyone, herself included.

So, Julie nodded at her old friend. She didn't invite her in but acknowledged her presence.

Charlotte took forever to speak. Instead, she stood in the doorway gently wringing her hands and opening and closing her mouth in a semi-parody of a fish out of water, which she was.

Julie and Charlotte had been friends since the 5th grade, when Julie had come to her rescue on the playground.

Charlotte had been the new girl in school and being pretty, she had immediately made enemies of the gang of mean girls, who were taunting her.

Charlotte had been embarrassed and had started to cry when she felt an arm go across her shoulders.

Looking to her right, there was Julie, coming to her rescue.

Julie hadn't said a word but just turned Charlotte away from in front of the girls, where she'd been standing, paralyzed.

Loudly, Julie had then proclaimed, "Come on! Let's go hang with the cool kids."

Since then (and up until the day of the wedding) Julie had thought they were best friends.

But best friends didn't have an affair with one's fiancé.

Best friends didn't pretend to be your best friend while sleeping with the man you were supposed to marry.

Best friends didn't take on the role of Maid of Honor when they had no honor.

Finally, Charlotte spoke, "Jules, I'm so sorry."

Julie calmly looked back at the woman, not saying a word.

"Please forgive me." Charlotte had started to cry a little.

Julie still did not speak. She just watched this woman who was now a complete stranger to her.

After several long moments, Charlotte spoke again.

"Well, are you going to say anything?"

She was finally starting to sound like her old self now – no tears mixed with slight impatience.

"No."

Julie didn't expand on her statement.

Charlotte stood there, silent.

When had Jules become so serene? This wasn't like her at all.

Usually, Charlotte was able to figure out her friend, but not at this moment.

Didn't Julie realize that Spencer had come onto her? **Spencer** had pursued **her**. It wasn't the other way around.

Didn't that mean anything?

Apparently not.

So, Charlotte felt the need to enlighten Jules on why this wasn't her fault – it was Spencer's.

But Julie wasn't having any of it.

When Charlotte started into explaining, Julie just held up one hand in a stop motion, which shut Charlotte up.

She'd never encountered this Julie before.

"I don't need or want any explanation from you, Char. Just leave my life. We're done."

Julie's calmness was so unusual that Charlotte thought she might be able to get around it, so she started explaining again.

And once again, Julie held up her hand.

"Please leave now." Julie indicated the hallway past where Charlotte was standing with just a nod of her head.

Then, Julie turned around and finished packing her things.

Charlotte stood in the doorway for just a moment longer and then turned and left.

Walking down the hall, she encountered various looks from her coworkers; disdain, rolled eyes, and shaking heads were the main ones.

What was she going to do now? Spencer had been distant recently, which also gave her pause.

Arriving back at her office, Charlotte closed her door and just sat at her desk, staring out the window.

The next visitor to Julie's door was fortunately someone Julie liked, and that conversation was much more pleasant.

Carrying her box of things to the elevator, along with a VERY nice severance check, she was given smiles, nods, and murmurs of "Good luck!" and "We'll miss you!" from her former coworkers.

As the elevator doors closed, her eyes misted over a little.

This part of her life's journey was now completely finished. Hopefully.

Chapter Thirteen

TURKS AND CAICOS – TAKE TWO

Julie's new job would probably last between six and eight months with the possibility of continued employment after this first assignment was successfully completed.

She had already secured an apartment condo on the islands and was looking forward to the change of pace. For sure, it was going to be very different from the energetic rush of New York City.

One of the upsides was that she didn't need to take any of her winter clothing with her to the islands. She was leaving most of her belongings in boxes until she knew more about where her life was heading.

Julie's second flight to the islands was sure different than the previous one had been.

Her "starting a new life" gift from her parents was a first-class window seat on the plane, as well as a new nature photography lens and professional accessory kit for her main camera.

She had waffled between packing her cameras in her luggage, carrying them onto the plane with her, or shipping them.

Although the equipment was heavy, she finally decided to carry it with her. Instead of schlepping the soft-sided camera case, which showed she was carrying something valuable, she was able to fit everything into a small roll-on bag, which looked just like everyone else's bag.

Bubble wrap surrounded everything inside the bag, with absolutely no room for anything else.

After checking her two other pieces of luggage at the curbside kiosk, Julie wheeled the carry-on and her favorite Michael Kors tote through security without too much hassle.

Of course, the camera equipment was inspected, but the TSA agent was gentle, which set Julie's mind at ease.

In fact, being a fellow photographer, the agent's admiration for her main camera was nice.

The roll-on bag was quickly repacked with care and she was on her way down the concourse toward the gate for her flight.

She had brought her Kindle (of course) and had loaded it up with travel books about the islands.

Julie didn't want to focus on the same shots as other photographers had done. She wanted to make her photos show the humanity and warmth of the locals that she had experienced.

She felt good that her flight was being used as research for her new job.

When the plane finally touched down on the tarmac, Julie felt energized. She could just sense that this move was the right one.

Julie pulled her rental car into the parking space just outside the door of her rental condo and took in the view.

Luckily, Julie and her parents had stayed in the UK several times over the years, and she had learned to navigate the roads as though she was in England – driving on the left side of the street, instead of the right side like in the United States.

When she'd been here last time, she'd found this place. The Inn at Grace Bay was perfect for her needs; not too crowded a property, yet enough people around her that Julie felt comfortable.

She had looked at a house for rent, but just coming from bustling NYC, the house had seemed a little too alone.

The rental agent who had shown her around the island had gotten her a great deal on the second-floor condo since Julie was looking at a long-term rental.

The building her condo was in was painted a bright cheery yellow. She wheeled her carry-on case behind her and pushed one of her suitcases in front of her. Her tote perched on top of the suitcase.

When she arrived at the staircase leading up to her condo, she realized her mistake. No elevators meant she'd have to drag her stuff up a flight of stairs.

There was no way she was going to be able to manage both of the bags at the same time.

Julie was standing there trying to decide whether to drag one of the bags back to the car or leave it at the base of the stairs when a masculine voice called from behind her.

"Need some help, love?"

Julie turned her head and saw a nice looking man smiling at her. He looked to be around her age with an open smile, wearing nothing but board shorts and flip flops.

He closed the distance between them and reached out to offer his help with the larger bag.

"I guess I hadn't thought this through," Julie explained her predicament.

He laughed and Julie relaxed.

"Actually, thank you." Julie decided to go with her gut reaction, which was that this man wasn't dangerous. "I'm on the second floor."

As he wheeled the suitcase up the stairs, he stated, "My name is Ian. Here on vacation."

"Hi, Ian. I'm Julie. Here to work."

Ian stopped on the second-floor landing and waited for Julie to indicate which way to go.

"I'm in unit 203, down at the end."

"Nice unit." Ian's voice had a slight accent to it. Very refined and faint.

Julie couldn't decide if it was English or Australian.

They arrived at Julie's door. She turned to Ian and held out her hand to shake his.

"Thank you for your help, Ian! I wasn't sure how I was going to work that."

He grinned back at her, "My pleasure, Julie."

He paused a moment before letting go of her hand.

"If you need anything else, I'm in 303, right above you."

"Wow. I'll bet you have a great view from there."

Julie considered the view from her unit to be outstanding. She could only imagine how much nicer Ian's view was.

Ian released her hand and stepped back.

"Well, I hope we run into each other. I'll be here for a few more weeks."

"I hope we do too, Ian." Julie's smile brought a grin to Ian's face.

"Excellent! Bye for now."

Julie watched as he sauntered down the landing back towards the stairs that lead up to the next floor.

Just as Ian reached the stairs, he turned around and waved at Julie, who was still standing there watching him.

Julie's face filled with heat as she realized she'd been gawking at this nice man's broad back. She waved back.

As he disappeared up the stairs, she rummaged in her tote for the key she'd picked up on her way from the airport.

Unlocking the door, she entered the space that would be her home for the next six months at least.

She set her bags in the entry hall and closed the door behind her, which automatically locked.

Looking around at the bright space, Julie felt her shoulders relax and a contented sigh escaped from her lips. This was going to work out perfectly.

She walked into the kitchenette and found a beautiful basket filled with goodies waiting for her. The attached note welcomed her and thanked her for her lengthy reservation.

Julie lifted out one of the wrapped packages of cookies and bit into the chocolate delight. While savoring the flavor filling her mouth, she opened the refrigerator door, not really expecting to find anything.

To her delight, there were several bottles of chilled water. She grabbed one of the bottles and carried it out into the open space towards her balcony.

She slid open the door and took in the view. Settling herself into one of the cushioned deck chairs, she opened the water and took a long drink.

Her unit faced the pool and further on the ocean could be seen in the distance.

The palms surrounding the pool area were swaying gently in the breeze. The sky was so bright blue it almost hurt Julie's eyes.

She got up and fetched her sunglasses from inside, along with another cookie.

Settling back down into the chair, she relaxed and just took in everything about her new home. Yep, this felt right.

Zan.

Where had that whispered thought come from? Julie's smile dimmed a little. She knew she needed to stop thinking about him, but every once in a while, he'd come to mind.

Where was he? Would she run into him? How was he doing?

Come on Julie, pull it together!

She shook her head and took another draw of her water, the cool liquid calming her thoughts.

Looking back out at the pool area, she noticed several people swimming or lounging on the blue covered pool chaises.

The blue umbrellas that matched the chaises added a nice balance to the shot.

Julie smiled at herself. Already she was setting up the shots she was going to take for the Chamber of Commerce's new ad campaign.

When she'd met with the Chamber members on her last trip, she had been able to present a couple of ideas off the top of her head, which had impressed them with her professionalism and sealed the deal to hire her.

Just then, Julie realized that she'd left one of her suitcases in the trunk of her car. She got up and headed back inside.

She smiled again at the calm light colors covering the walls of her place.

The soft warm mint color matched perfectly with the splashes of the Caribbean blue of a lamp, a couch pillow, and a bookcase.

The warm vanilla cupboards in the kitchen completed the color palette of the open floor space.

Her bedroom was painted the same soft warm mint with clean white bathroom and closet doors.

The ceiling fans throughout the unit were made of a woven rattan and painted a neutral beige.

Overall, it was a soothing environment.

Julie grabbed her room key and her car key and headed back out to retrieve her last piece of luggage.

As she got to the base of the stairs that lead up, once again she heard a male voice.

"We have to stop meeting like this."

Julie laughed as Ian came down the stairs and grabbed the handle of her heavy suitcase.

Julie hadn't been looking forward to dragging it up to her room, but she needed to get unpacked.

"Thank you again!" Julie smiled at him as he arrived at her door.

"I think you owe me now." Ian's return smile was broad.

From any other man, that remark might have sounded a bit sinister. However, Ian's tone was friendly and playful.

"How about if I buy you breakfast one of these days?" Julie thought that would be a good trade for all of his help with her luggage.

"It's a deal." And once again, Ian held out his hand to shake.

Julie put her hand in his and shook.

"Just name the day." Julie felt very comfortable in Ian's presence.

"Let's give you a couple of days to settle in. How about Tuesday?"

"That sounds good! See you Tuesday morning, just not before 8:00 am, please."

Ian's laugh was almost contagious.

"That late, eh?"

Julie scoffed and replied, "Oh, so you're an early bird?"

"Just to hit the beach for a run."

"Okay. How about breakfast after your run?"

"How about you join me on the run?" Ian's eyebrows lifted with the question.

Julie didn't even hesitate. "Actually, a run sounds good."

And with that, Ian gave Julie a little salute and jogged back over to the stairs, heading down them this time.

Julie dragged her bag into her condo and shut the door behind her.

Hmmm. Maybe this trip will include some possibilities. Male possibilities.

Is Zan a possibility?

Julie stopped dead in her tracks.

Stop it! Just stop it.

And once again she was able to push Zan's image to the back of her mind.

For now ...

❧

It was Monday morning at 9:00 am and Julie was standing in front of the doors to the building where the Chamber of Commerce was located.

Taking a deep breath and shifting her presentation bag to her other shoulder, Julie opened the door and entered the lobby of the building.

The room was cool and dark.

And empty.

And silent.

Julie walked over to the only piece of furniture, which appeared to be a reception desk of sorts.

It looked like no one was working there; no coffee cup, no lamp, no notes, not even a phone.

Okay. Now what?

Julie looked around for an elevator and failed to see one.

Hmmm

However, she did spot the set of stairs and headed towards them.

The building felt hollow as Julie ascended the stairs.

Reaching the next floor, Julie walked down the tiled hallway, her heels making the only noise she could hear.

Finally, at the far end of the hall, she spotted the Chamber's door with the official seal on it.

The spread-winged pelican at the center of the seal made Julie smile. She had seen so many since arriving back on the island.

She knocked once and waited.

Nothing.

She knocked again, a little louder.

Again nothing.

Trying the doorknob, she found that it was locked.

Hmmm.

Just then, she heard someone coming up the stairs at a pretty good clip.

A young woman in a gauzy pink top, shorts, and sandals reached the top of the stairs and turned down the hallway towards Julie.

"Hello! You must be Julie!" The young woman's voice had a beautiful island lilt to it.

"Hi! I am."

"Sorry I'm late. I was just getting a coffee when I remembered your appointment with us."

She reached the door and unlocked it with a key hanging off her vividly painted parrot key chain.

Julie followed her into the office, where the young woman proceeded to turn on the lights and open the wooden blinds to bright sunshine.

The room was minimalistic except for huge paintings of the island's main tourist spots.

The paintings covered every wall and brought an aliveness to the room that Julie appreciated. The art was amazing.

"Let me introduce myself." The young woman held out her hand.

"I'm Selina." Her smile was brilliant, and her eyes matched the clear green of the waters surrounding the islands.

"I'm so glad to meet you!" Julie's smile matched Selina's own as they shook hands.

"We've spoken over the phone and now I have a face to go with the voice."

Both women realized they had met a friend.

"Please have a seat!" Selina gracefully motioned to the lime green couch that faced two matching chairs with a rattan coffee table situated in the middle.

"Let me show you ..." Julie started to unpack her presentation bag in preparation for showing Selina her work.

"Oh! No. I'm not the person you'll be working with. I'm just the office manager."

Selina's small wave of her hand indicated she thought what she did was less important somehow.

"I have never met a successful office that did not have an energetic and resourceful person as the office manager. So, don't give me that. I know better."

Selina threw back her head and laughed at Julie's wagging finger.

"Well, I always thought so and I agree with you completely!"

And with that, their friendship was forged.

Julie found out that the eight Chamber members were meeting the next afternoon and wanted to see what she'd come up with as a marketing campaign.

"What time do you want me here?"

"The meeting is scheduled for 4:00 pm, however please keep in mind that we are all on island time."

At Julie's look of noncomprehension, Selina continued. "Although we try to meet on time, there are no points lost if you run a little late – or early for that matter. I imagine our clock is a little looser than the one you're used to in New York City."

"I actually welcome that! Although I am punctual, the pressure of being on time can make for a hecticness that is unpleasant." Julie's expression made Selina laugh.

"I think you will fit in just fine."

"Now, I have a packet that the Chamber has put together for you, showing you our past marketing strategies; some of which worked and some of which didn't. They would like for you to take a look and put together something for them."

Julie was silent for a moment. Why hadn't they given her these things earlier when they first decided to hire her?

She'd spent hours creating the presentation she had brought with her today.

Selina seemed to pick up on Julie's hesitancy.

"I'm sure whatever you've already developed will fit nicely. Look over the previous things the Chamber has done, and I think you'll see that you're fine."

Julie relaxed a little with that and had the realization she was feeling NYC type pressure to perform.

This is certainly a big change in my life!

The ladies finished up with Julie stating she would be there tomorrow and Selina giving her several local restaurants she thought Julie would enjoy, as well as where to buy groceries.

Back out on the street, Julie waved goodbye to Selina and got back into her car. Where she immediately rolled down the windows.

The inside of the car felt like a sauna!

She grimaced when she felt a drop of sweat run down her back.

I hope I acclimate soon!

Julie laughed when she realized she had worn way too much clothing for this morning's meeting.

Yep, dark slacks, low heels, and a jacket over a blouse were way too much for island couture.

Maybe a shopping trip for some lighter and looser clothes was on the agenda for today.

And with that thought, Julie's outlook got even brighter.

Chapter Fourteen

OF ALL THE GIN JOINTS IN ALL THE TOWNS IN ALL THE WORLD

Julie noticed that everything seemed to slow down around mid-afternoon. All the shops were still open for business, but there was less foot traffic on the sidewalks and the stores were less crowded than they were earlier.

She was very happy with the new wardrobe she found; lightweight fabrics and bright colors, yet professional looking. Her NYC fashion palate just didn't fit in here.

Nope, sleek dark colors and black leather boots weren't seen anywhere.

Julie was standing at the checkout counter with a couple of pairs of sandals that matched most of her new closet items.

The shoes weren't flashy with jewels or sequins, In fact, they looked slightly dressy and professional. One pair was a soft beige with darker piping and the other pair was vanilla white.

Both had heel straps and felt supportive, yet they were surprisingly comfortable and airy.

Mental note – keep up with the pedicures!

As she handed the clerk her card, she heard a deep male voice from behind that stopped her dead in her tracks.

"Just visiting again?"

Julie took a breath before turning around.

Zan stood there, looking better than ever.

"Hi." Julie's voice didn't fail her completely, but almost.

His smile seemed pleasant enough, but his eyes seemed to burn a hole in her. The heated intensity was almost too much to confront.

And time stopped for both of them.

Zan had been starting to think he'd imagined his reaction to Julie while she was a guest on his boat.

But now he knew without a doubt that if anything, he'd underestimated what she did to him.

Julie could only gaze back at Zan while she prayed her heart would start again.

After what seemed an eternity, the clerk asked again, "Miss?"

And the spell was broken.

Julie smiled at Zan and turned back to the clerk, trying to will her blush into submission.

"Thank you." Julie put her card back into her wallet and turned back to Zan.

"Actually, I have a job here." Julie was pleased with her almost-normal voice.

"Wow!" Zan enjoyed watching all the emotions that flitted across Julie's face.

If anything, she was more beautiful than he'd remembered.

"Yes! For the Chamber of Commerce. I'm working on their new marketing campaign."

And with that statement, Zan's whole future looked even brighter to him.

Just then a female voice called, "Zan, honey. What do you think of this one?"

It only took Julie a split second to recognize the beauty gliding over towards them, holding out a scarf in one hand.

The walking mermaid. The perfect walking mermaid. The perfect walking mermaid that had legs longer than Julie was tall.

Once again, Julie's heart thudded to a stop in her chest.

"Oh, hi! I remember you! On Zan's boat – right?"

Why did her smile have to seem so friendly? Why did she have to seem so nice?

Julie gave a slight mental grimace before answering.

"Hi. Yep, that was me."

Then she turned back towards Zan, the earlier light that seeing Zan had lit in her dimming to just a flicker.

"Well, it was nice seeing you again. Take care of yourself."

And with that, Julie managed to give a small smile and headed towards the shop's door.

"Julie! Wait!" Zan loped over to catch up with her.

"Actually, I have to run. I'm late." Julie was trying to hold everything together in what she hoped was a nonchalant manner.

Zan's eyebrows drew together in puzzlement.

What had just changed?

"Where are you staying?"

Julie couldn't believe he was continuing their conversation as though his girlfriend wasn't right there in the store.

"I really have to run. Didn't notice how late it was!" Julie threw a small smile at Zan as she rapidly exited through the door and made a beeline for her car.

Zan just stood there, frozen inside the shop's door, and watched Julie get into her car and drive off.

What the heck had just happened?

Julie managed to get herself back to her condo, parked her car, and practically ran up the stairs and through her front door.

Shutting it behind her, she leaned her head back against it and closed her eyes against the hot tears that she'd managed to hold at bay until she got home.

Stupid! Just stupid, Julie!

She berated her reaction to seeing Zan and then her bigger reaction to seeing *The Mermaid* with him.

She and Zan didn't have anything! There was no relationship there. So why did she feel betrayed?

She was just tired – yes, that was it. She was tired from moving to the island. She was tired from the earlier meeting at the Chamber.

And hungry! That was all it was. She just needed some food and then maybe a nap.

With that decision made, Julie set her purchases down in the living room area and headed to the kitchenette for something to eat.

Luckily, she had stopped by the Gracebay Gourmet yesterday and had stocked up on food for the coming week.

The store had a wonderfully extensive deli section, so Julie had purchased several meals to go along with a couple of sandwiches she couldn't resist.

After choosing the turkey wrap, she poured a glass of lemonade and took everything out to her balcony area.

The jasmine-scented breeze was cooling on her skin, and she started to relax after a few minutes.

Luckily, her mind also shut down and she was able to just eat and watch the palm fronds sway with the soft air.

After filling her stomach, Julie was able to go lie down and swiftly fell into a deep sleep.

Once again, Zan was feeling clueless about women. He rubbed his hand over his head in frustration.

He really wished he knew what had happened with Julie.

It was so good to see her again. And the fact that she said she had moved here had made him feel happy enough to grin.

And then, out of nowhere, Julie's whole demeanor shifted, and she was gone in a split second. And she hadn't told him where she was living.

Zan could only shake his head in confusion.

After dropping Monica off at her condo, Zan had headed back to his boat. He didn't mind helping his friend when she needed help.

Zan and Monica had grown up together. Although some people had thought they were an item, they weren't. There was just no spark there.

Besides, Zan thought Monica's love life was a little too chaotic for him. She'd fall in love hard for the guy and put him up on a white horse.

Then, she'd become upset when he turned out to not be perfect, and she'd dump him; usually to the guy's total bewilderment.

Then she would come crying to Zan and he'd give her coffee if she'd been drinking. Or food if she hadn't. He'd listen to her story about the latest guy and all his imperfections – in Monica's mind.

One time, Zan had tried to reason with her.

Nope. Not a good idea.

Monica had stormed out of Zan's house and he hadn't heard from her for several weeks.

Several blessedly quiet weeks.

Then, they had run into each other at one of the myriad fundraising events that Zan attended on behalf of his family's company.

Monica had been on the arm of the son of one of Zan's dad's business friends. A nice enough guy, but Zan could see from Monica's expression that the new guy's suit of armor was starting to tarnish a little already.

Sure enough, a week later Monica showed up on Zan's doorstep in tears.

Zan wished she'd let him help her with some advice, but he'd learned from his earlier experiences trying just that; it didn't work.

Today's shopping trip had been a pleasantly even-keeled afternoon – right up until he'd spotted Julie in that shop.

Their conversation had started out pretty good. In fact, he'd picked up from Julie's initial response that maybe something was starting up between them.

And then, out of the blue, Julie had shifted gears and practically run from the shop.

After some consideration, Zan had decided that he was going to take up Julie's hesitancy as a challenge and try to see if there was something more between them than just a couple of days at sea.

First thing was to find where she lived.

And that could be easily handled by placing a call to the Chamber. After all the donations his family had send towards the Chamber, one new address of one new employee shouldn't be too hard to get from the Chamber President.

And it wasn't!

Selina was more than happy to give Julie's address and phone number to Alexander DeKeurge, since the number wasn't unlisted.

Chapter Fifteen

BEAUTY AND BRAINS

Jaimee had hit a brick wall – for the first time in her life.

Making decisions was usually easy for her. But now, when it really counted, she couldn't decide.

Come on, Jaimee – focus!

She turned to her father, sighed, and nodded.

"Okay, Dad. You win."

"Thank you, Jaimee." Mr. DeKeurge smiled with pleasure. "You've made the right decision."

Jaimee turned to Ana, who was standing in anticipation. "Well, it looks like we're going to be moving some furniture!"

And with that, the decision was set in stone.

Jaimee hadn't wanted to move into the CEO's office. She'd wanted to leave that space for her dad. But he'd made a good argument.

If she was going to be running the DeKeurge Foundation, she needed to be in the CEO's office. The employees as well as other business leaders would expect it.

If she didn't move into the CEO's office, it would possibly create rumors that she was the new CEO in name only.

And Mr. DeKeurge wanted to retire. He didn't want to be approached at parties and events for a "quick word" from another business leader.

He wanted to enjoy watching his daughter grow the family business into an even bigger and better enterprise. He was looking forward to traveling with his wife on vacation, not on business.

It had gotten to the point that all business meeting rooms had started to look the same, no matter which country he was visiting.

"Miss Jaimee, I'll get the movers in here this afternoon." Ana was beaming from ear to ear.

"What's with the 'Miss Jaimee,' Ana? I've always been Jaimee to you." Jaimee's eyebrows raised in question at her new administrative assistant. She'd already had the conversation with her that she was no longer going to be referred to as the CEO's secretary.

Ana was very happy with her new title "administrative assistant," as well as the pay raise that came with it. The family already paid her more than most other companies paid their CEO's assistants, but Ana was not one to say 'no' to their generous offer.

"In private, I will refer to you as 'Miss Jaimee.' In pubic, you are 'Ms. DeKeurge.' I want to show you the respect you deserve as our CEO."

At Jaimee's slight frown, Ana continued.

"This will also set the tone for the rest of the employees and other business people you will be dealing with."

Jaimee's dad nodded his head in agreement.

"Jaimee, why do you think that Ana has always referred to me as Mr. DeKeurge, and not my given name?"

Mr. DeKeurge and Ana smiled at each other as though they were friends sharing a secret.

"I'd never paid any real attention to it. It has been that way my entire life." Jaimee realized that she'd never noticed that detail before now.

"Jaimee, when I took over the reins of this company, I was younger than you are now. My father complained that vendors and employees were still going to him for decisions after he'd retired, and he wanted the only person still coming to him for advice to be me."

Mr. DeKeurge was making an important point to his daughter.

"So, he explained to Ana and me that she should start referring to me as 'Mr. DeKeurge' to help build me up in the eyes of the people I needed to lead. That it would set the tone for the rest of the world."

Ana chimed in, "So, I started referring to your father as Mr. DeKeurge with others and in person. And it worked!"

Jaimee admired the simple solution her grandfather had implemented.

"Okay, so why not 'Ms. DeKeurge' instead of 'Ms. Jaimee?'"

At this question, both Mr. DeKeurge and Ana looked around the room in feigned indifference.

It only took Jaimee a few moments to realize the reason.

"Is that in case I get married and take my husband's last name as my own?"

Mr. DeKeurge rubbed his hands together as though done with something, and headed towards the door, calling over his shoulder, "I just remembered an appointment I had scheduled for right now. I'll stop by later tomorrow to see how things look, Ana. Jaimee, come by for dinner tonight. Your mother would love to see you. She's preparing all your favorite foods in celebration of your new position in the company."

143

And with that he had made it to the hallway door, shutting it behind him as he left.

Jaimee's gaze turned towards Ana at the same time Ana headed towards her connected office area.

"I'm heading out for lunch now, Ms. Jaimee." Ana grabbed her purse and got to the outer door before Jaimee could reply.

As the door shut behind Ana, Jaimee just stood there shaking her head in amusement. Well, it didn't look like she was going to have much say in how Ana referred to her. She'd known the woman her whole life and knew that to argue beyond this point would only waste valuable company time.

Jaimee smiled and looked around the CEO's office – *her* office!

The view from the huge window behind the desk was amazing. Being on the top floor, she could see across the few buildings between their location and the ocean. The azure sky was expansive and dotted with white clouds that moved leisurely out to sea on the zephyrs that were a continual part of the island.

Jaimee hugged herself and gave a quick smile of pure joy. She'd achieved it! She was now running the Foundation. Her dream since she was in her teens.

Her smile dimmed slightly at the thought that flickered through her mind just then.

And you're still alone.

Elliott, the guy she'd been dating, was never around and an empty house and bed sure could be lonely...

Chapter Sixteen

SO CLOSE...

Julie thought her lungs were going to burst.

She'd thought she was in pretty good shape. But trying to keep up with Ian was quickly disabusing her of that idea.

Ian turned around in front of Julie and ran backwards along the beach with a grin plastered across his face.

"Come on, slowpoke. Stretch those legs."

Julie gave up, stopped running and leaned forward, hands on knees, to catch her breath.

Ian's face quickly turned to concern as he ran back to where Julie was inelegantly sucking wind. He placed a hand on her back.

"Are you okay?"

Julie just rolled her eyes at him as she tried to calm down her pulse and breathing.

Finally, after several more deep breaths, Julie stood up straight and wiped the back of her hand across her forehead to keep the sweat from running into her eyes.

She was sure she looked horrific.

Ian thought she looked great.

"Sorry. I didn't realize you were so out of shape." As soon as the words came out of him mouth, Ian realized his mistake.

Taking a step back, he raised his hands as though warding off an attack, even though Julie was just standing there staring at him, still attempting to calm her pulse rate and breathing.

The look on his face was priceless! Watching Ian try to squirm out of his last statement, and all that it might potentially bring on, made Julie break into a grin.

"At ease, Ian. I won't bite." Hands on hips, Julie was able to take a few steps in a circle while trying to keep her legs from cramping up.

Ian tried a charming smile. "That did not come out correctly. It is NOT what I meant to say."

Julie continued walking in the circle, occasionally glancing over at Ian.

Ian switched to pleading. "Please forgive me. Sometimes I am not as eloquent as I'd like to be."

Julie raised one eyebrow.

"Okay, okay." Ian had started walking backwards in front of her. "Let's change that. Sometimes my words are not the right ones."

"Better." Julie was enjoying Ian's antics to try and win her back over.

Then Ian stopped walking and Julie had to also stop or she would have run into him.

"Jules, I'm so sorry. I do not think you are out of shape." His eyes did a rapid skim over her body, down and back up. "Not at all."

Julie pretended to have to think about what he'd said.

"How about if I buy you breakfast to make up for my conversation blunder?"

Julie laughed out loud. "Okay, Champ. You're on. I accept your attempted apology."

"Attempted! I thought it was pretty good!" Ian relaxed and smiled.

"Pretty good doesn't cut it when you tell a gal that she's out of shape."

"You know that is not what I meant! Now you're just being mean." Ian's grin couldn't hide the fact that he was thoroughly enjoying their verbal sparring.

Just then, Julie took off running back the way they had come. Albeit slightly slower than before.

Ian just enjoyed the view.

After returning to their respective condos, showering, and dressing, Ian and Julie met at the top of the stairs at the same time.

"Okay, to make things up to you, I am taking you to the best breakfast place on the island."

"I would have assumed nothing less!" Julie quickly descended the stairs to the ground. "Not to mention, you're driving."

"Of course!"

Ian drove them along the northern part of the island heading up to the island's eastern area of Grace Bay.

The restaurant itself was located poolside at one of the tourist resorts. At first, Julie was a little let down, thinking it would be overpriced and underwhelming.

But she was wrong.

After being seated at a table out on the deck overlooking the pool, they were immediately served a great cup of coffee.

Okay, so far so good. Julie's opinion was starting to change.

When her breakfast arrived, it smelled delicious. Fried eggs. Applewood bacon. Banana pancakes. Breakfast potatoes. It was perfect.

Ian's choice matched her own, but with an added side of grits.

"Grits? I wouldn't have taken you for Southern." Julie had never actually had grits before and was curious. "May I take a bite?"

Ian nodded his approval around a mouth full of pancake.

Julie reached over with a spoon and scooped up some of the creamy mixture.

She opened her mouth to accept the food and closed her eyes, ready to savor the taste.

And then promptly opened her eyes and swallowed.

"It tastes like mushy rice. Hardly any flavor!" Julie sounded disappointed.

"You didn't wait for me to add the butter and sugar!" Ian couldn't contain his reaction to Julie's disappointment with her first taste of grits and grinned.

"I think it's sort of like eating oatmeal. Not much flavor until you add the brown sugar, cream, raisins, and walnuts."

"I had heard so much about grits that I was expecting something more exotic. Or at least, spicy."

"Nope. It's plain old comfort food."

"Okay. I can see that. I guess you had to grow up with it for it to be comfort food." Julie took a bite of her bacon and sighed.

"Now, this is what **I** call comfort food."

Ian laughed at Julie's expression of pure contentedness.

Their breakfast continued in that wonderfully relaxed way that some meals go. Good food, good company, easy conversation, great ambiance, and no deadline.

"You haven't told me yet what you do, Ian." Julie's head tipped to the side in question.

Ian's smile stuttered slightly and then came back full wattage. It had happened so quickly that Julie thought she might have imagined it.

"I inspect things."

Well that wasn't very enlightening, Julie thought.

"What kind of things?"

Ian paused as thought trying to make up his mind. Finally, he replied, "People."

Now it was Julie's turn to pause. What did *that* mean?

They sat silently for a moment, then each took a sip from their coffee.

Julie broke the silence with, "You do know how creepy that sounds, right?"

Her one-sided smile softened her words.

Ian chuffed out a laugh, "Yes. Yes, I do."

"I'll explain." He sat back and rubbed his hands over his face while pulling his thoughts together.

"You see, companies hire me to investigate people they, well, need investigated.

"Let's say a new CEO is taking over a company. Sometimes someone on the Board of Directors might want to ensure that person can do the job, so I basically check out that person to see if there are any red flags that might pop up."

"Wow! That sounds intriguing." Julie was impressed. She'd thought that Ian was a middle-management kind of guy, not a spy of sorts.

"So, how do you do it? Is it boring, like going through lots of paperwork or do you actually do some James Bond-ing?" Julie was starting to view Ian through a different lens now, and she wasn't sure if she liked the new view.

"Honestly?"

When Julie nodded, Ian continued, "A little bit of both."

Again, Julie paused and then asked, "So, are you here on vacation or work?"

Ian repeated, "A little bit of both."

The silence stretched out between them while Julie gathered her thoughts and Ian tried to read from her changing expression what she was thinking.

After what must have been a full minute, Julie said, "Are you here to investigate me?"

Thank goodness Ian hadn't been taking a drink of coffee at that moment, or he would have spit it out all over the table.

"Good Heavens, NO!" Ian laughed at the thought.

Julie seemed to relax a little.

"Well, that's good news – eh?" Her small chuckle broke the tension that had developed between them.

Ian reached across the table and covered one of Julie's hands with his own.

"I'm so sorry you thought that, Jules!" He squeezed her hand. "My job has nothing to do with you at all. That said, my vacation definitely has become something to do with you."

She smiled back at Ian and they finished breakfast.

The rest of the meal was relaxing for both of them and they headed back to their condos.

After dropping Julie off at her door, Ian went back up to his condo, settled in at the desk, and opened his laptop.

Typing in "DeKeurge Industries," Ian dove into researching one Rebecca Jaimyson DeKeurge.

Julie woke up from her afternoon nap refreshed and clear-headed. She had enjoyed breakfast with Ian. He was easy to be around.

What about Zan?

Oh, good grief! She needed to get ahold of those wandering thoughts! Zan was obviously already in a relationship with The Mermaid, as Julie had been mentally labeling the woman.

And that woman obviously fit what he was looking for; tall, thin, and drop-dead gorgeous.

Then why had Julie felt something from him on the boat?

She sighed and then shook her head and straightened up.

Time for a little jaunt around the island; scope out some of the scenery for research for her new job.

Julie gathered up a sandwich and a bottle of water to take with her. Then, grabbing her camera case from inside the front closet, she set out to explore.

After driving north from her condo, Julie decided to turn left and headed west on Leeward Highway. That road lead to a fork.

Julie chose to turn right onto Millennium Highway instead of towards the airport. The highway led her to Malcolm Rd, which finally lead her to a dirt road, which lead to a stunning private resort with its own private beach.

Wow! Julie made a note to check with the Chamber about this place. It covered over 18,000 acres of nature reserve and 1/5 mile of private beach.

From there, Julie slowly headed north over another dirt road to the island's North West Point Marine Natural Park. She found a parking space even though there were several vehicles already there.

Climbing out of her car, she grabbed her camera and headed for the beach.

She found out later that it was locally referred to as Malcolm's Road Beach.

The wind, which had earlier been gentle, was picking up and the sun was becoming dimmed by a swiftly incoming bank of clouds.

As Julie's feet met the soft white sand, she noticed there was a group of about 20 people heading towards her and the exit.

One of the women was holding a large cardboard check with a lot of zeros on it.

The group seemed happy yet were moving swiftly to beat the inbound rainstorm.

Just as the woman with the check spotted Julie and smiled, Julie heard her name called from somewhere in the group.

Zan couldn't believe his eyes. There was Jules, walking slowly toward him.

Zan was surrounded by several other local business owners as well as a couple of representatives for the island.

Everyone had on casual shorts, slacks, or skirts as well as different brightly colored tee-shirts emblazoned with a silk-screened sea turtle and coral reef.

"Jules!" Zan waved his hand.

Julie couldn't believe her eyes. There was Zan, in the middle of the crowd.

Well! Of all the beaches on all the shores on all the islands in the Caribbean, she had walked onto the one beach where he was at.

Julie just stopped walking and stared at him.

Zan weaved his way through the crowd, many of whom had taken an interest in seeing who he was waving at.

He finally arrived in front of where Julie was cemented to the sand.

"Hi!" Zan's smile showed he was happy to see her.

Julie just stood there, basking in that smile. Even her heart hummed a little bit.

Finally finding her voice, she answered with a smile, "Hi, Zan."

The last few people to hurriedly make their way past the couple just smiled and waved at them as they left.

Soon, it was only the two of them on the beach, standing about four feet from each other.

The only sounds were the seagulls calling out and the ocean waves starting to be pushed onto the sandy shore.

The sun was blocked out completely by the clouds that were threatening rain at any moment and the wind was getting stronger.

"It's good to see you, Jules." Zan still smiled.

"It's good to see you, too, Zan."

"I've been meaning to contact you." Zan was about to explain about getting Julie's number from the Chamber.

And just then, the skies opened up as though a hatch door had been swiftly thrown wide and the couple were instantly drenched.

They both turned and ran back towards the parking area, Julie trying to keep her camera safely dry under her shirt.

Arriving at the two cars left, Zan quickly opened the passenger door of his Range Rover and Julie climbed into the seat.

He then shut the door behind her, and the instant silence engulfed her.

Wow! Captaining a fishing boat must pay really well. The soft leather seating cradled her.

Zan yanked open the driver's door and jumped in, shutting the door behind him.

They were both grinning from the sudden downpour and how bedraggled they both were with all the rain.

Zan reached behind his seat and pulled up two beach towels.

Julie immediately used the one he'd handed her to wipe down her camera, which had surprisingly remained relatively dry.

Julie turned to thank Zan for the towel when she noticed his eyes were on her chest area.

Looking down, she gasped as she realized that the top half of her blouse was plastered to her and the water had pretty much made all cloth invisible.

She glanced over at Zan to see him vigorously rubbing the towel over his face and head.

Was that a groan from him?

Geez, Zan. Get a grip! Finally, he felt he could maintain his composure enough to look at Julie again – in the eyes this time.

He lowered the towel and rubbed it over his arms and chest, while he threw another smile at her.

Now it was Julie's turn to stare.

Nice.

She already knew what it felt like to be held in those strong arms against that broad chest, from when she'd cried on his boat and he'd comforted her. It seemed like a lifetime ago.

"How's your camera?" Zan nodded towards the equipment nestled in the towel that was now higher and covering Julie's chest area.

"Oh. Um. I think it's going to be okay." Julie tried to pull her wandering thoughts – and heating hormones – back under control.

"Good."

The rain was washing down over the windshield as though a fire hose was being directed on it. The harsh wind was lashing at the car, buffeting it slightly in spite of the vehicle's sturdiness.

"Nice car!" Julie admired the console area with the touch screen mounted in the middle of it.

"Thanks! It's one of the company cars."

"Your fishing boat is a company?"

Zan paused for a moment, realizing that Jules didn't know about his family's business. Did he want to tell her right now?

Over the years, Zan had discovered that many times new relationships had instantly changed when the lady he was with found out that he wasn't just a boat captain; that actually his family had a fortune.

He really didn't want that to happen with Julie. There was just something about her that rang true for him. Yet, he didn't feel ready to let her know that he had billions at his disposal.

In fact, he'd been on the beach that morning handing over a donation check to the local sea turtle conservation society.

They were a small but extremely dedicated group and the DeKeurge Foundation had donated to them these past six years.

Zan paused before answering Julie's question.

"No. My fishing boat is just me. But I'm on the Board of Directors for one of the other companies here on the island."

He then pointed to the emblem on the front of his shirt next to the turtle.

Zan knew that was misleading, and he didn't feel particularly good about doing it.

"What does the company do?" Julie had noticed all the brightly colored shirts with the same logo on them that everyone had been wearing on the beach.

"They're a conservation group dedicated to bringing back up the lowering numbers of turtles in the area."

Zan paused for another moment.

"In fact, this group is actually the reason I sailed my boat closer to that pirate boat during our sailing trip. They had a turtle caught in their net, or so they wanted us to think, and I couldn't ignore it."

Julie's heart warmed even more towards Zan when he explained about the turtle.

Wow. He truly had a soft heart under his sometimes façade of gruffness.

"I understand." Julie's smile quickened Zan's pulse.

He was able to push down the uncomfortable feeling of lying to her about his wealth – for now.

As fast as it had hit, the rain suddenly stopped. The wind died down and the clouds opened to let the sun peek through.

The effect was stunning.

"Wow! That was fast!" Julie was amazed at the weather's speed of change.

"I know. It never gets old and I've lived here my whole life."

Zan opened his car door and stepped out. The breeze that swept in and over Julie felt warm and dry.

Julie opened her door and also got out.

Facing away from Zan she held the front of her blouse away from her body so that air circulated to help dry out the thin cloth.

Zan came around the back of the car, fanning his shirt, also drying it out.

Their eyes met and they laughed out loud at their actions.

"Do you want to head back to the beach? You didn't get any pictures, yet, did you?"

"I think I'll do just that. Good idea!"

Julie reached back into Zan's car and grabbed her camera. After placing the strap around her neck, she pressed the on-button and checked that everything was working correctly.

Yep, everything was in order – except maybe her composure. She was trying to be upbeat and nonchalant with Zan.

A pretty tall order at this particular moment.

"Is it okay if I join you?"

Zan was also striving for casual and shoved his hands into his front pockets and shrugged.

"It's a public beach." Julie thought she should have won the Tony for "acting unaffected."

But when she saw Zan's smile start to dim, she added, "I'd love to have you join me."

Zan grinned again and with a wave of his hand indicated for Julie to go before him on the trail leading to the beach.

When they reached the sand, they both took off their flip-flops. Zan carried both of their footwear in one hand while Julie turned in a slow circle, looking for a good shot.

Which was not possible to miss – everywhere she spotted was a good shot.

This was so different than shooting in the city. There, she had to be aware of background debris, possible pedestrians walking between her and her photo subject, and all the extra lighting necessary in some shoots.

Here, there wasn't a bad shot!

The next 30 minutes went by fast and Julie got more than she needed for shots of this beach.

The sugar white sand, dotted with dark slabs of rock, led down to the clear aqua water.

"I need to get some underwater equipment. I'll just bet it's gorgeous out there." Julie indicated the ocean in front of them.

"I can take you to some of the most beautiful areas around the island on my boat. If you get out a little further, you can see all the marine life around this island's own great barrier reef. It's stunning."

Zan's pride in the island was evident to Julie and her opinion of him notched up even further.

"I'd like that very much! Thank you." Julie's joy was evident in her face, which made Zan smile even bigger.

"Yes. We could either snorkel or scuba, whichever you prefer."

"Oh." Julie's voice faded.

"You scuba, right?"

"Um. Not for years. I had one lesson at a summer swim camp when I was 13. I really don't remember much about it at all."

"Not a problem, Jules. I'm a certified dive instructor. I'll teach you." Zan held his breath while waiting for her reply.

"Really?" Julie's face brightened up. "That would be wonderful, Zan."

And with that, their day on the beach ended with a promise for the future.

Driving home from the beach that early evening, Julie couldn't stop smiling to herself. Not only had she gotten some great shots for her project, but she'd spent time with Zan again.

Being around him made her happy. Except when she thought about The Mermaid, his girlfriend. Julie shook her thoughts away. That's all right. We're just good friends.

Nothing to get upset about.

Nothing to look at.

Nothing there at all.

Julie sighed and grabbed her camera bag from the passenger seat of her car and headed for the stairs.

Once again, at the top of the stairs, was Ian, as though waiting for her.

"Hey! I was just heading out for an early dinner. Want to join me?"

Julie smiled up at him. Now here was an uncomplicated man. A friendship that didn't confuse her. She knew they were friends, and only friends.

"I'd love to! Just let me put this away and do a quick freshen up."

"You look great just as you are." Ian's open smile made Julie smile back.

"I'll just be a second."

Julie ran up the stairs past Ian and headed for her door.

"I'll wait right here for you!" Ian called to her while making a show of looking at his watch.

Julie laughed at him and entered her condo.

Looking in the mirror, Julie was surprised at her decidedly windblown hair, which looked good!

Her face had some pink in it from the sun that day and her hair seemed to like the humidity and had naturally softened into a casually pretty look.

Hmmm. Maybe this island living was going to be really good for her!

She quickly used the bathroom, dabbed on some lip gloss, grabbed her purse again, and headed back out the door. All in less than 5 minutes. Not bad!

As she headed towards Ian, she saw him deliberately close his eyes and pretend to be asleep standing up. When she laughed out loud at his play, he opened his eyes and smiled at her.

Their dinner was easy-going and pleasant for both of them.

Although Julie could sense that Ian might want to take their relationship further than friendship, she didn't feel any pressure from him.

And Ian was bemused by the fact that he was starting to view Julie like a kid sister instead of a potential girlfriend.

Hmmm.

This was certainly different for him, and he was actually getting charmed by this new way of being around a female. It was refreshing for him to just relax without some game plan in motion.

They arrived back home and after saying goodnight, Julie and Ian each went into their own condos. Julie found a good movie to watch, while Ian opened his work file on the DeKeurge Foundation and made plans...

Chapter Seventeen

I'm Not Threatened!

"What?" Jaimee couldn't believe what she'd just heard.

She'd just kicked off her heels and was padding around her condo in slippers, phone in one hand, late-night cookie in the other. She'd gotten home from another board meeting and was exhausted.

So, of course, now was the time that Elliot decided to finally call her back.

She'd been waiting all day for his return call. And now that she'd let her defenses down, it just made it that much harder to deal with him.

"Elliot, what do you mean?" Jaimee tried this time to keep her voice level.

"Jaimyson, don't make this more difficult." Elliot sounded miffed. As though Jaimee was the one who had started this conversation.

"Okay, now you're referring to me as Jaimyson. What's up." Jaimee didn't even try to hide her consternation at this point.

After a sigh that could have been heard in Jamaica, Elliot spoke. "We've been through this before. The Board is not happy that your father has named you as his successor. They wanted Alexander."

And there it was – out in the open – what Jaimee had been sensing all evening at the meeting. Even though it had not been stated outright, she had perceived it.

Not from everyone there. Just from two of the older gentlemen who had been with the company for decades, and apparently now from her boyfriend.

Maybe it was time to make that "ex-boyfriend."

"I'm sorry you feel that way, Elliot. But I have no say in the appointment and neither do you. We all know that the company has had it in writing since the company was founded that the current CEO has the authority to name his replacement."

"That's just the point, Jaimyson. *His* replacement. The company has historically placed the eldest son in that position."

How had she ever thought Elliot was the guy for her.

"Barefoot and pregnant? Hanging on your arm at dinner engagements? Speaking when spoken to?" Jaimee couldn't hide her disgust.

"Now you're just being petulant." Elliot actually sounded offended.

Eyeroll.

"No, Elliot. I am facing reality. News flash: we are no longer a couple. I no longer want you in my life." Jaimee was slightly surprised at the relief she felt saying those words.

She strolled into the kitchen and poured herself a small glass of port. She'd earned it today.

"Well, you see, Jaimyson, that's just it. I am in your life and will remain so. If you've forgotten, I am on the Board of the DeKeurge Foundation."

Jaimee paused while heading back into the living room.

"Is that a threat, Elliot?"

"No. Just a statement of fact."

She just stood there, silent, waiting for the other shoe to drop.

And it finally did.

"I intend to see you removed as your father's replacement."

Hm-mm?

"Elliot, you know that Zan doesn't want the job."

"That's true." Elliot paused for a moment. "But I do."

Wow! Didn't see that one coming.

Again, silence.

Jaimee was proud of how cool and bored her voice finally sounded, even though she was vibrating in anger.

"Bring it on." And with that closing statement, Jaimee ended the call.

Letting out a huge breath, Jaimee sat down on her cream-colored linen couch before her knees let go.

She knew that legally there was nothing Elliot could actually do about it.

She'd never heard or seen that defiant and hateful side of him before. It was a little unnerving to realize they had been a couple now for almost two years and she'd never known he could be like that.

He'd seemed so charming at first.

They'd met at a fundraiser for the Foundation and had seemed to hit it off immediately.

Now, she wondered if his interest in her romantically had always been a sham just so he would be hired at the Foundation.

Small things that she'd noticed before, but hadn't paid much attention to, now made sense. His frequent trips off the island on weekends to "visit his family."

Jaimee realized she hadn't ever spoken with or met his so-called family. It had always been planned for some time in the future.

The fact that he would end off a phone conversation if she happened to walk into the room right before he'd face her and turn on the charm.

His lack of romantic gestures. Sure, she'd received flowers on her birthday and Valentine's Day. However, they were always delivered by the florist in front of all the office personnel at work, never personally over dinner.

She thought she should feel worse right now, but all she felt was relief and a slight discomfort with her inability to have spotted him sooner. Usually she was pretty good at sizing up someone.

Jaimee wondered if she should call Zan or her father and inform one of them about the conversation she'd just had with Elliot. She checked the wall clock and realized how late it was.

No, it could wait until tomorrow.

"Have you found anything yet?" Elliot sounded irritated.

"No, nothing."

"Well, have you *tried* to find anything?" Elliot gave a sigh of annoyance.

It took everything Ian had to not climb through the phone and grab his client by the throat.

"You're welcome to fire me anytime you want to if you don't think I'm doing this job right."

Elliot paused for the moment. He knew that Ian's investigation company was one of the best for the money.

"No. Sorry." Elliot reined in his impatience with Ian's lack of findings about anything in Jaimyson's past that would help him convince the Board to get rid of her and put him in her place.

"I apologize, Ian. I'm just under some stress." Elliot tried to make his voice carry some warmth in it.

"I understand." Even though Ian didn't really, he wanted to reassure his newest client.

"I promise I'll contact you immediately if something shows up before our call next week." Ian actually thought he wasn't going to find much on this Rebecca Jaimyson DeKeurge.

So far, everything he'd seen had been above-board to the point that she sounded almost too good to be true. However, his client thought there must be something there, so he would continue to look.

"Thank you, Ian. I appreciate the work you're doing. Good night."

With that, Elliot closed his phone and just stood there, frozen like a statue. Suddenly, in a rage, he threw his phone at the gilded mirror above the mantle in his front room.

The shattering sound brought a smile to his face. A smile that would have caused anyone noting it to draw back in either fear or disgust. His grin looked feral.

He lost the smile for a moment when he realized that he'd need to get a phone replacement tomorrow – again.

Chapter Eighteen

NOT JUST A PRETTY-FACED SAILOR

Julie was elated! Her meeting with the Chamber had gone perfectly that morning. They liked the shots she'd gotten so far.

They were also happy with the promotional plan she had outlined to them that morning.

When she'd mentioned that she was going to acquire an underwater lens for her camera, they had offered to pay for it!

Wow. Nice group to work with.

And what a difference from Spencer's group in NYC. She remembered having to complete extensive forms in order to get reimbursed for even simple costs at times. Although she had enjoyed working with her fellow employees as well as the clients, her memories were mostly disappointing now.

Julie swore she would never get involved with someone at work again. Or a client for that matter. Just "keep things simple sweetheart" – her dad's mantra.

She'd spoken with her parents last night and everything was going very good at home. They were thrilled for her new adventure, mainly because **she** was thrilled with it.

Her mom was still being mom, but without the stiffness that used to accompany her words.

In fact, last night her mom had started to say something about Julie's wardrobe after Julie had shared with her about her new clothing purchases. And then, Julie's mom had caught herself, given a small laugh, and told Julie it sounded so different to her.

Yep, changes were happening.

And now, Julie had an additional assignment from the Chamber.

She was scheduled to shoot an event in four weeks. Apparently, the island was holding the annual awards banquet for all the volunteers who help with the different charities in the Turks and Caicos Islands. It was a very big deal. And very formal – at least the banquet itself.

Julie was informed that each island would send representatives and award winners via ferry or plane the morning of the banquet.

Before the actual banquet, there were several scheduled photo shoots that they wanted Julie to cover as well as the main event itself. They'd given Julie the photo shoot locations and she was looking forward to scoping them out beforehand.

Julie was brought out of her musings by her phone ringing. She didn't recognize the number.

"Hello?"

"Hey, there." Zan's rich voice seemed to tumble into her from the phone.

Okay. That was definitely a reaction.

"Hey!" Julie didn't know what to say after that.

"Are you free for lunch? I mean, can I take you to lunch?" Zan hoped his voice didn't betray him. He was trying to sound casual when he was really hoping she'd say yes.

"Um – sure." Julie's hesitation had to do with the fact that she and Zan hadn't discussed his girlfriend yet and Julie wasn't sure if she could be just friends with this man she was so attracted to.

"You have other plans already?" Zan's hopes took a dive.

"No." Julie decided that the new her wouldn't be hesitant to just say it.

"Won't your girlfriend disagree with you taking another woman to lunch?"

"Girlfriend?" Zan was not understanding. "What girlfriend?"

Julie silently rolled her eyes at Zan's seemingly denseness.

"You know. The Mermaid."

Silence.

Julie figured now that he'd been found out, lunch would be cancelled.

Finally, Zan found his voice again. "Mermaid? Okay, now I'm lost."

Julie sighed to herself. Was Zan really that dense or had she misread something?

"The tall, beautiful gal who was on your boat and also with you at the shop downtown?"

Zan actually had to think for a moment. Then it hit him. Julie thought he and Monica were an item!

"Monica? You mean Monica?" Zan couldn't contain the undercurrent of laughter in his voice.

Julie frowned to herself. **Had** she misread their relationship?

"Um. Yeah. I guess so." Julie's hesitancy made Zan smile.

"Monica and I are very old friends. She's like a sister to me. We grew up together."

"Oh." That was all Julie could think of to say.

"Oh?" Zan couldn't contain his grin. Now he understood Julie's hesitancy. And that meant that maybe now there wouldn't be any back off from her.

Julie realized that she had fallen into an old habit. Assuming something and then making a decision based on her assumption.

Well, that changes right now.

From now on, she would ask questions and find out before deciding anything.

Julie thought to herself. *Alright! A better me.*

She let out a breath and smiled before asking, "Where are you taking me?"

Zan let out a breath and smiled before replying, "Do you like seafood?"

❦

Their table was sitting in about four inches of sea water!

Zan took Julie to a hut-type restaurant on the beach. There were tables available inside the spacious hut building, outside the building on the covered deck, or further outside in the sand at the edge of the crystal blue ocean.

They chose one of the ocean side tables, and now, 45 minutes into their lunch, it was surrounded by water as the tide came in.

Which explained to Julie why she had seen a boat just sitting on the beach a little further out. When the tide comes in, the boat then floats.

Interesting way to "dock" a boat!

Julie and Zan had finished eating, and rather than swimming inland sometime within the next hour, they decided to vacate the table at this time. They waded through the water and carried their plates and glasses up to the deck where one of the servers grabbed them with a smile.

"The ocean does not cover the tabletops if you want to stay out there for a while." His smile was contagious and Julie and Zan both responded with their own.

"No. Thank you anyway. We're done." Zan took out some cash from his pocket and peeled off a couple of bills, handing them to the server.

"This should cover our meal as well as leave a nice tip."

The server's smile got even bigger, if that was possible.

"Yes, it does. Thank you!"

Zan turned around and took Julie's hand in his and lead her back to his car. This vehicle was his own; a Jeep with a large open area in the back, ready to carry supplies for his boat.

It was kept up just as nicely as the company car had been, but Julie thought it definitely looked more the style for a fishing boat's captain.

After they climbed into Zan's Jeep, they headed back towards the dock where Zan had his boat.

When they arrived, Julie saw both Pierre and Robert working on the deck. They both looked up when Zan's car parked dockside.

Upon spying Julie get out, both of the men broke into broad smiles and headed over to the edge of the boat to help her aboard.

"Miss Julie!"

"How are you?"

"It's so good to see you!"

"When did you get back?"

They spoke over each other while helping her aboard. Julie just smiled at the warm welcome while Zan grinned and shook his head at the change in the two men.

One minute, they were working diligently, but not particularly joyfully, and the next minute, upon spotting the woman that each of them felt they had saved, they were falling all over each other to help her onto the boat.

"Hi, guys!" Julie gave each of them a hug.

Zan joined them and everyone just stood there smiling at one another for a moment.

Pierre was the first to speak.

"Can I get you anything? A drink perhaps?"

"Oh, thank you, Pierre. But I'm stuffed. We just finished having lunch." As Julie turned to look over the boat, she missed the look that both Robert and Pierre gave Zan.

Zan pretended not to notice their questioning looks.

"Wow, guys! The boat looks great!"

Julie turned to Zan.

"Can I look around?"

"Be my guest, Jules." Zan was proud of the way he made sure his boat was kept sparkling, now that Robert had finally learned some responsible habits.

Zan's older sister was going to be thrilled when Robert went home eventually, and he had to admit that Pierre had a lot to do with the changes in Robert.

At first, the two men really didn't seem to like one another. However, after the pirate incident, they had both expanded in ways that suited them.

Robert seemed to grow up a bit and Pierre seemed to loosen up and talk more.

Zan was happy for both of them.

Observing their joy at seeing Julie, Zan had the thought that maybe he should invite back Mr. VIP and his assistant, Marc, for some sort of reunion.

However, the thought of Marc being around Julie again, didn't sit so well with Zan.

Dude! Get over it.

Zan decided to ask Julie at some time about her and Marc. Later. Right now, he wanted to see her expression when she saw the new cushions he'd installed on what he now considered her reading area.

Just then, she arrived back at the aft deck. "New cushions! Zan they look great!"

Zan knew that he reacted to her praise a little more than he probably should have, but he was so happy she noticed the upgrade. Especially since he had her in mind when he bought them.

Sort of an unstated hope that he'd see her again.

His grin said it all. "I'm glad you approve!"

"Let me show you what else we've done!" Robert felt pride in the way his uncle's boat was coming along with the upgrade.

Pierre put a hand on Robert's shoulder to stop him.

When Robert turned to Pierre, about ready to demand "What?" Pierre just did a side head nod towards Zan, who had moved closer to Julie.

Robert's expression of confusion turned to understanding. "Ah. Actually, there's work I ..." Pierre nudged Robert in the side with his elbow. "**We** ... actually there's work that **we** need to finish."

And with that the two boat-hands took off for the other end of the boat, grinning.

Julie and Zan had a hard time containing their laughter about Robert and Pierre's obvious antics at leaving them alone.

"Sorry 'bout that." Zan was standing very close, hands on hips, smiling into Julie's eyes.

She couldn't catch her breath. When she finally inhaled to answer him, she had to stop. He smelled so good; a mix of male and sunshine.

Zan's eye darkened as he watched Julie's humor change to heat, and he took the last step separating them, leaving only inches before their bodies touched.

He couldn't resist what he'd been wanting to do all day.

Julie reached up her hand and softly placed it on his chest.

Zan wasn't sure if she was stopping him or ... her fingers then curled into his shirt.

No, not a stop.

He reached an arm around her back and closed the already short distance between them. His other hand raised to her face and gently caressed her cheek while his thumb guided her chin up, so her mouth was closer to his.

With eyes open, he lowered his lips to hers, waiting for her reaction.

Upon the first touch of their lips, Julie seemed to melt into him as her eyes gently closed.

Zan's body caught fire at her surrender to his kiss. His arm tightened around her, pulling her tightly up against him.

Julie raised her hands to Zan's broad shoulders and clung for support as their kiss deepened.

After what seemed an eternity, or maybe it had just been a moment, Zan lifted his mouth from Julie's and rested his forehead against hers as they both caught their breath.

"Um. That was really nice." Julie's voice was thin and breathy.

Zan chuffed out a laugh. "Nice. I can think of so many more words than 'nice.'"

Julie leaned back in Zan's arms to look at him directly, her smile saying it all.

He couldn't resist and leaned in for another kiss from her soft mouth.

This time was it was a gentle, loving declaration from his heart.

She felt so right in his arms. She fit perfectly. Like she'd been made just for him.

And Julie's heart responded to it. Her thoughts were spinning and yet were warm and comfortable.

Zan's arms felt like home to her. She'd never experienced that feeling before. Certainly, never with Spencer.

The gentle kiss was starting to deepen again when they stopped and reluctantly drew apart as Robert and Pierre, speaking much louder than usual, approached the back of the boat.

"So, are you guys going to hang around here all day?" Robert was trying to not-notice the scene he and Pierre had walked into.

Zan grabbed Julie's hand and drew her towards the front of the boat, where Robert and Pierre had just come from.

"Nope. You guys can resume your work here. We'll get out of your way."

Robert and Pierre just grinned as Zan and Julie moved forward.

Robert's phone rang just then, and Pierre shook his head in mock disapproval as he heard Robert answer with "Hey, Baby! Thanks for calling back. Are you free tonight?" Robert just threw a grimace at Pierre as he waved him off and turned his back on him.

Pierre was envious of the young man's energy and stamina; working hard all day and then heading out for the island nightlife in the evening. After a long day on the boat, all Pierre wanted to do was relax with a nice cut-crystal glass of whichever high-end spirit he had available ... and write.

It was Pierre's secret passion – to become a published author. He had a great story swirling in his head that he just knew would make for a great film or TV movie. So, he had started putting it to paper right after the pirate attack. He didn't know if he was any good or not, but he didn't have a choice – he had to write.

Zan had settled Julie onto one of the newly upholstered chaise lounges and had stretched out on the matching one next to her.

Julie sighed and nestled into the softness of the cushion. This was turning out to be her all-time favorite day.

Zan couldn't help but catch glances at Julie's legs. Well-shaped and firm, Zan wondered how they would feel wrapped around him ...

Whoa! Cool it, man! Zan silently sighed at his wandering thoughts.

This wasn't just about heat. This was about Julie.

This was about the way she had stayed in his mind even after she'd left the island.

This was about the way his heart had leapt in his chest when he's spotted her in that store downtown a few weeks ago.

There was definitely something going on here, more than just physical. Although, the physical was outstanding, Julie had touched something in his heart that he thought had died when his ex-girlfriend had left him a few years back.

And now he felt the tender yearning again to have a wife and children in his life. He'd always wanted to be a dad. He could picture his family on their private beach, enjoying the sun and warm water.

He remembered when he'd brought it up once again to Claire about getting married and starting their family. She'd laughed as though what he'd said was silly.

"Alexander, I have no problem with marrying you. In fact, I'd love a nice engagement ring on my finger. But I've told you, I'm not sure that I want children." She'd said it with such a soft tone that her words didn't seem like she really meant them.

So, Zan had continued their relationship, thinking that one day she would agree with him.

Luckily, some little voice in the back of his head had warned him to get this one item straightened out before committing to their engagement. Especially since Claire had already stated her ambition of being married to the CEO of the DeKeurge Foundation.

However, that hadn't kept it from hurting when she'd left the island with someone else and not a word to him.

Now, Zan thought maybe his ego had been hurt more than his heart.

He reached across and claimed Julie's hand in his.

When she turned her head towards him and smiled, he knew that he'd fallen hard for her.

She just felt so right.

Maybe his dream would work out after all.

Chapter Nineteen

TRUTH OR DARE?

Ian ran into Julie that morning.

"Hey! Haven't seen you in a while! Everything good?"

"Hi, Ian!" Julie grinned at him while carrying a couple of bags of groceries up the stairs. It was becoming normal how Ian always seemed to be on the landing.

"Here, let me grab those for you." Ian reached out and hooked his hands through the plastic bags, taking from Julie's hands.

"Thank you! But you know you don't have to do that, right?" Julie was glad for his help, however as the bags were getting heavier the longer she carried them up the stairs.

"So, where have you been?" Ian's open grin was always good to see. It was nice having a neighbor she could trust.

"Well, if you must know," Julie opened the door to her condo and Ian followed her inside to the kitchen area, setting the bags on the counter.

"I've been working on the advertising campaign for the island! They are really happy with my work." Julie's started putting the groceries away in cupboards and the refrigerator.

"Jules, that's great!" Ian was so happy for his friend. He leaned against the counter and watched her work.

"PLUS ... I've been taking some outstanding underwater pictures out at the reef."

Julie was proud of the way she'd learned scuba diving so fast from Zan. It had turned out to be much easier than she'd thought. Especially with Zan as her diving partner. He was a natural-born teacher.

"Wow! Okay, I'm now officially impressed." Ian had never seen Julie more happy.

"So! How about you and your life? Anything new?" Julie shut the last cupboard and turned towards Ian.

Ian's eyes clouded over for a split second, but not before Julie noted his mood change.

"Ian. Spill it."

He sighed and pulled out one of the kitchen chairs to sit down.

Julie sombered and joined him at the table. Apparently, her friend was having some difficulties.

"I don't know if I told you or not, but I'm here to do a job."

Julie's eyebrows lifted. "Yes, you briefly mentioned it. Something about investigating a person for a company."

"I don't normally talk about my work, since it's usually confidential."

He paused as though making a decision." "But I think I can tell you without giving away any secrets or violating the confidentiality of the contract."

Now he **really** had Julie's attention. "I'm all ears."

"I'm starting to feel like I should have vetted my client better. Something feels off. And I'm not happy with the situation."

"Well, if you have reservations about your client, you're probably right." Julie trusted Ian's instincts. He seemed competent and probably knew what he was doing.

After a moment, Ian's face relaxed. "You're right! I'm going to move forward as though he can't be trusted to have told me everything."

Ian seemed to make a decision. "I'll look at this with fresh eyes."

He looked across the table at Julie and smiled.

Ian covered Julie's hand with his. "Thank you, Jules! You are a true friend."

And with that statement, their status as good friends was secured.

⸙

Ian opened his laptop and took a brand new look at the file on Rebecca Jaimyson DeKeurge. She didn't look quite as menacing without the filter of his client's words overshadowing the woman. Hmmm. Time to research the client.

⸙

"Hi, Julie! It's Selina at the Chamber of Commerce!" Selina's voice was a smooth blend of cheerfully relaxed and professional.

"Selina! How did you know I wanted to talk with you?" Julie was glad to hear from her new friend. She had some questions about the campaign.

Selina's laugh made Julie smile as she sunk down into her couch.

"You go first! How can I help?" Selina's smile easily came through the phone.

"I had a question about the rest of the islands. Has the Chamber made a decision yet on which ones I need to shoot? I think I've got everything for Provo that will be needed."

Julie was already speaking like a natural islander. The island of Providenciales where she was now located was referred to locally as Provo.

"Not yet." Selina laughed again. "Girl! You need to slow down even more. Remember? Island time. This isn't New York."

Julie exhaled when she realized that she'd started to slip back into her old city mode; shoulders stiff and tenseness in her stomach.

"You're right, Selina! I just automatically do that. It's just that I want to do the best job I can."

"And you are! The Chamber is very happy with what they've seen so far."

Julie relaxed completely. "Thank you. I'm glad to hear that."

"In fact, the reason I'm calling is to verify the special shoot happening before the Volunteer Banquet. One of our local philanthropic foundations will be presenting a very large check to the island volunteer organizations.

The man who will make the presentation is one of our local favorite people as well as the son of the CEO. He's expected to take over the company this year!" Selina couldn't conceal the admiration from her voice.

"Wow! Sounds like a really great job – handing out huge checks!"

Julie smiled at the mental picture she'd gotten of a short, balding 40-something smiling at the camera, surrounded by thankful people. It would make for good promo for the island.

"Just send me the details and I will ensure great photos for you." Julie relaxed even more. This was going to be a very fun event.

"I'll email them right now." Julie could hear Selina's fingers on her keyboard in the background. "Done!"

"Thank you! I'll mark my calendar."

"So..." Selina's voice denoted a change in topic. "Meet anyone interesting yet?"

Julie grinned at Selina's question. Over the past few weeks, she had tried to introduce Julie to various people around the island, hoping to help her make friends. Julie had now met every cousin that Selina claimed.

"As a matter of fact, I have!" Julie thought of Zan and the day they'd had yesterday snorkeling again in the azure waters that surrounded the island. It had been relaxing as well as giving Julie the chance to get more underwater shots with her new camera. Julie had fallen in love with the brightly colored fish and beautiful underwater world Zan had introduced her to.

"He's a local and runs a fishing boat."

"Nice! Instant transportation between the islands." Selina was happy for Julie.

"Yeah. And he's not so hard on the eyes, either."

Selina laughed at Julie's comment. Yep. Julie was doing just fine.

"Speaking of which, I need to go get ready for another day on the boat. He's taking me to another snorkeling spot he thinks will be even more interesting for me. We're heading out to the Grand Turk island."

"Oh! You'll love that! It is truly some of the best diving in the world." Selina's joy was apparent in her voice.

"I'm looking forward to it!"

"In that case, I'll let you go. Have fun!" Selina disconnected.

Julie set down her phone, a grin spreading on her face. She was really looking forward to another day with Zan. Their friendship seemed so easy and natural. And the underlying heat between them didn't hurt either!

After that one searing kiss on his boat, Zan had cooled his jets a little trying to slow things down so he could savor learning all about Julie. And Julie had been in agreement with the unstated change of pace.

That didn't mean that the feel of his fingers brushing against her skin as he helped her strap on the diving tank didn't cause all sorts of wonderful reactions in her body. The fact that they'd relaxed the physical side of their relationship a little only seemed to make it more intense when they did touch as their feelings for each other grew.

Julie got up from her couch and headed to the shower. Time to get ready for another wonderful day with Zan.

The next couple of weeks brought a calmness and stability to Julie's life that she'd never experienced before.

She had a great job where she was valued.

She'd developed friendships with the locals where she shopped as well as at the Chamber. Selina felt like a new best friend.

And Zan.

Zan was becoming important to her. At times, she felt like she'd known him forever. Their humor was so similar that if something funny happened when they were out and about, they could just look at each other and know what the other one was thinking.

Zan valued Julie's viewpoint on so many things when he shared his dream of a fleet of fishing boats. She understood his passion for his own business as she recognized the same need in herself with her photography.

Julie felt safe and wanted when she was with Zan. Sometimes the heat in his eyes just took her breath away. He didn't even need to touch her to create a wonderfully warm effect in her.

They had kissed another time that happened suddenly for both of them.

They had just come up out of a dive and had stripped out of their gear on the back deck of his boat. Julie was drying off her hair with a towel, laughing at something Zan had just said.

When he'd stopped laughing, Julie had turned towards him and saw that heat in his eyes.

It was mesmerizing and seemed to pull Julie towards him.

When she stood right in front of Zan, she put a hand on his chest, her eyes moving from his eyes down to his lips.

That's all it took.

Zan's arm wrapped around her waist, skin to skin, while his other hand cupped the back of her head as he moved in, his lips on hers.

This was no soft kiss. This was thing that movies were made about; that stories were written about; that women dreamed about.

Julie could only cling to Zan's shoulders, his arms holding her up as her knees literally weakened.

Their kiss went on forever, their lips only parting as they both drew in breath.

Just as Julie thought Zan was going to kiss her again, his dark eyes locked on hers and he relaxed his hold around her waist and at the back of her head and leaned in, placing a soft lingering kiss on her forehead.

Julie couldn't help but sigh at the emotion that soft kiss conveyed.

"Hungry?" Zan's voice was deep with warmth.

"Oh, yeah." Julie's voice trembled in the aftermath of that kiss.

"I meant for food?" Zan couldn't contain his smile at Julie's reaction.

"Oh! Yes. Of course." Julie seemed to come to her senses and smiled back at Zan.

"I think we should get some lunch." Zan still hadn't removed his arm from around her waist.

"Um. I think that would probably be best." Julie didn't move away.

"I'm glad you agree." Zan's hand now rubbed up and down her back.

"Food." Julie's hands left his shoulders and rested on his chest.

"We have to go ashore, since I gave Pierre and Robert the day off." Zan slowly removed his hand from Julie and stepped back a little.

Julie picked up the towel that she'd dropped on the deck and finished removing some of the water from her hair, then quickly fluffed it up with her fingers to air-dry.

"Sounds good to me."

Zan pulled up the smaller anchor they'd used in the shallow waters to keep the boat secure while they'd dived, then walked toward the stairs leading up to the bridge.

As Julie felt the engine rumble beneath her feet, she grabbed the bathing suit cover-up she'd worn earlier before their dive.

She smiled as she remembered the look on Zan's face when she'd taken it off, showing the small two-piece suit she was wearing. He had obviously approved of it by his slowly spreading smile.

His reaction had given Julie a feeling of womanly power. She felt very feminine and slightly seductive. Although that feeling was new to Julie, it just felt right when it happened with Zan.

Julie climbed to the bridge and joined Zan, looking towards the beach they were heading for.

Were those donkeys on the beach?!

"Oh, Zan! Look!" Julie pointed at the shaggy haired animals.

Zan laughed at Julie's reaction of little-girl joy at the equine pack in front of them. She was delightful to watch. Again, this woman just being herself charmed him completely.

As he pulled the boat up next to the dock that stretched out from the beach into the water, Zan looked forward to lunch with Julie.

Zan tossed the front dock line onto the dock while Julie jumped down from the boat to secure the line around the cleat which was attached to the edge of the dock.

Zan grinned at watching Julie. She looked like an old hand at sailing; knowing just what to do.

He tossed the second line from the back of the boat and Julie secured that one perfectly, too.

Julie looked up at Zan for confirmation that she'd done it right. She then gave a jaunty salute after Zan nodded his approval of her work.

"I must admit that I've never had a cuter crew member working with me before." Zan jumped down onto the dock and took Julie's hand in his.

Before he turned to walk towards the shore, he leaned down and planted a kiss on the top of Julie's nose. Then with a smile of satisfaction he turned and headed towards lunch with Julie, cradling her soft hand in his.

Julie sighed quietly while her heart swelled up with feelings for this man. His large warm hand wrapped around hers in a protective way that Julie hadn't realized she'd been missing all her life.

She realized that up to this point, she'd unconsciously kept her guard up. Never letting it completely down, even within her own family.

Julie liked the fact that she was starting to realize things about herself that she was fixing, along with spotting the things she really liked, but had never given herself credit for.

Before now.

As they got closer to shore, Julie tugged on Zan's hand to move faster. She wanted to go over to where the donkeys were.

Zan could only laugh with delight watching Julie's face light up when one of the animals spotted Julie and started plodding towards her.

Zan knew the beast was looking for a treat, but he didn't think that Julie realized that.

"Oh! He's looking for food!" Julie turned towards Zan with her remark.

Okay! She did know. Zan liked that she was so observant. One more thing to add to his list of why Julie was perfect.

"I'll run up there and get something. Be right back." Zan enjoyed the fact that this gave him the chance to play hero in a small way.

He approached the outdoor bar which was located next to a wooden deck covered with tables and chairs for seating.

The bartender knew Zan and had no problem handing him a couple of carrots that he kept behind the bar just for the purpose of letting tourists feed the donkeys.

By the time Zan arrived back at Julie's side, the donkey had walked over to her and she was rubbing his shaggy head.

The donkey appeared to be enjoying the attention, leaning its head towards Julie, and slowly leaning into her.

Julie's laughter at the donkey's motions to get closer to her made Zan grin. He understood completely! Getting closer to Julie has been on his mind a lot recently.

Zan looked up and saw some of the others in the herd starting to pay attention to them.

"I think we need to head up to the restaurant if we don't want to be inundated by the others. I only brought two carrots!"

Julie followed Zan's line of sight and made the same decision.

"Bye, big fella!" She gave the donkey a last knuckle rub between his ears.

Zan and Julie joined hands and headed up the walkway towards the bar. Zan looked over his shoulder to make sure they weren't being followed.

They weren't.

Julie's new friend was lumbering back towards the others, content with the affection and food he'd gotten from her.

The rest of Julie and Zan's day only added to their growing connection to each other.

Chapter Twenty

SAYONARA SWEETHEART

Julie checked her appearance in the mirror on the wall again. She wanted to look professional, yet slightly island-casual. The charcoal light-weight slacks, low-heeled shoes, and soft coral top were perfect. She would put on the matching jacket when she got into the air-conditioned ballroom where they were holding the awards banquet that evening.

The day couldn't have gone any better. Julie's shots of the various attendees went smoothly and fast enough that no one got impatient with posing and smiling for her camera.

It had helped tremendously that Julie had scoped out the various locations over the past couple of weeks and had already lined up which angles at each location were best for the shots the Chamber wanted her to get.

This evening would be a little bit formal at the big hotel's main event space for the presentation of the awards. Julie had already checked out the spacious room a couple of days earlier, so she knew what the lighting would be like and had brought everything she needed to ensure the pictures would turn out flattering to almost everyone on stage.

The Event Manager had already set up the staging and seating earlier, so Julie was able to work out where she would be located for the shots.

Thank goodness for long-range lenses, camera stands, and a raised platform at the back of the room.

Julie grabbed her camera bag and purse and headed out to her car.

Although it had been a long day so far with all the shoots around the island, she felt pumped about tonight's event. Selina had explained to her about the importance of the award attendees to the islands' growth and prosperity.

Since tourism was the main income for the islands, there was so much that being successful depended upon. Such as sustaining the natural coral reefs around some of the islands that made up the Turks and Caicos. The wildlife was important. Balancing the islands' natural charm with modern updates that most tourists expected.

It was a delicate balancing act that most visitors did not take into account.

The people who made all that happen were gathering together this evening at an event to commemorate their selfless work, which went most of the year unacknowledged.

There was also the large check being presented from The DeKeurge Foundation.

Yes, tonight was a very big deal for the Turks and Caicos Islands and their people.

Julie used the valet parking at the event space and after receiving her claim ticket, carried her equipment into the venue.

She was an hour early, which would give her plenty of time to get situated and setup to produce terrific shots for the Chamber tonight.

The Event Manager greeted her as she crossed the marble entryway and headed towards the elevators that would take her to the banquet room.

"Can I help you carry anything?" He seemed excited yet slightly distracted with everything he had to coordinate to make this evening successful.

Julie was glad her only job was the photography.

"Thank you!" Julie handed him one of her duffels as they stepped into the elevator.

Upon entering the banquet room, Julie stopped and openly showed her admiration of all the work that had gone into the set-up.

"This is gorgeous!"

The Event Manager stood a bit taller and gave Julie a wide smile.

"Thank you! I think it's the best we've ever done!"

"It is stunning. Great photos are going to be easy to get with this incredible background.

The hotel had turned the room into an underground grotto-like space. The tables were covered with sea green linen cloths.

The centerpieces were sculptures of various underwater creatures nestled on a scattering of various blue, green, and gold colored metallic confetti as well as small battery-operated tea lights.

The walls were covered with shimmering strands of what looked to be metallic seaweed; the special hidden lighting on the walls made the strands look like they were swaying under the ocean.

The place settings at each table consisted of a large gold charger plate, gold flatware, empty aqua-hued wine and water glasses, awaiting beverages to be poured into them, and a linen napkin that matched the tablecloth and was held secured by a take-home gift for each attendee -- a ceramic circle with the event's logo engraved on it.

Julie got everything set up and had practiced some shots when more people started to arrive. The next ones to enter the room were Selina along with a tall handsome man in a tuxedo.

Wait ... what was Zan doing here? Julie hadn't expected to see him here and dressed like the cover of GQ Magazine!

He looked great!

He also had a large cardboard rectangle with him.

"Hi!" Julie called over to them and waved.

Selina turned, and spotting Julie, walked over to her for a hug.

"You look great!" Julie admired Selina's floor length gown which accentuated her slender curves.

"So do you! Very professional." Selina held Julie out at arm's length to take in her working outfit.

Julie and Selina both turned towards Zan who had been frozen to the spot, ala a deer in headlights.

So many thoughts were running through Zan's mind that he couldn't focus. Why hadn't he realized Julie would, of course, be taking photos at tonight's event?

And why hadn't he told her yet about his financial status?

They had been getting along so well, that he'd forgotten to even mention his family's foundation. It had just never come up!

Well, no time like the present!

"Uh, hi! Hey, Jules." He approached Julie and gave her a kiss on the cheek.

Julie couldn't figure out why Zan was acting so odd.

Selina just stood there glancing between the two, back and forth, sort of like watching a tennis match.

"It's good to see you, Zan. I didn't know you were attending tonight." Julie smiled a tentative smile at him, which he returned with a half-smile half-grimace.

"Um. Yeah. I'm here tonight." Zan sort of nodded towards and held up the large piece of cardboard in his other hand.

Now, Julie was looking between Zan and Selina. Something was truly off.

"Mr. DeKeurge, doesn't she know?" Selina's perplexed voice set off some warning signal in Julie.

"Know what, Selina?" Julie was still confused as to what was happening.

Both women turned towards Zan.

Who just stood there.

Silent.

Finally, Julie was able to breathe out a question, "Zan?"

Zan inhaled and exhaled. Then he turned towards Selina.

"Could we please have a moment?"

"Of course! I'll be at the presentation table up front." And with that, Selina shot a quick look at Julie and walked away.

Zan reached out and took one of Julie's hands in his free one as he took a step closer to her.

Julie smiled at his touch and looked up into his face.

"There is something I totally forgot to tell you that I should have told you quite a while ago."

Now Julie was starting to seriously worry. Was he married? Was there someone else?

"Zan, just spit it out. I'm a big girl. I can take it." Julie steeled herself to hear the worst.

"I have money."

Crickets.

Finally, Julie found her voice, "Okay. So do I."

Zan cleared his throat.

"Yeah, but not like I do."

"What's that supposed to mean, Zan? I don't understand."

Julie was truly perplexed with trying to figure out where this conversation was heading.

"Lots of money."

Julie shrugged and gave a tentative smile, "Good?"

"Yes, it's good. But I should have told you before."

"Okay, Zan. That's fine. My family has money, too. It's not a crime."

Zan shifted from one foot to the other, then lifted the check so Julie could read it.

Julie's mouth dropped open.

"Uh. Okay. THAT kind of money." Julie thought for a moment and still couldn't find anything wrong with it.

"I'm not understanding, Zan. Why is this a problem?"

He just stood there, silent. Almost willing Julie to understand without him having to state anything.

Finally, it started to dawn on Julie.

"Did you not tell me because you were afraid of my reaction?"

"No."

Silent beat.

"Okay. Did you not tell me because you are embarrassed that you have that much?"

"No."

Again, quiet.

Julie became irritated.

"Okay, Zan. Then tell my why? Why didn't you tell me? I'm not understanding."

Zan let go of Julie's hand and rubbed the back of his neck in frustration.

He didn't want to say it out loud because now it would sound awful.

Julie just continued to stare at him, willing him to speak.

Zan's voice actually cracked a little, "I was afraid you would like me for my money and not just for me."

Now it was Julie's turn to be silent as she processed what he'd just confessed.

After shifting from one foot to the other, Julie asked, "Is that what you really thought I would do?"

"No! Not at all. At least, not after I got to know you." Zan at least had the good grace to blush as he continued.

"And by the time we'd moved along is our relationship, it just never seemed to come up. Jules, I'd actually forgotten that I hadn't told you until I saw you standing here tonight."

Julie remained silent, trying to understand why this was becoming so upsetting to her. It didn't make any sense, but she was really becoming angry with Zan.

"So, you waited to tell me until you could find out if I was a gold-digger or not? You wanted to make sure I wasn't after your money? Does that about sum it up, Zan?" Julie's voice couldn't have sounded colder.

"Well, if you put it like that, it sounds bad."

"That's because it is bad. You didn't trust me. In fact, I'm curious, Zan." She spit out his name like it was a knife stabbing through his heart.

"Do you trust me -- yet? Obviously not, since you hadn't told me until you had to."

Now Julie felt like she was climbing up onto her high horse with indignation.

"How much longer would you have kept it a dirty little secret from me, Zan?"

"Zan, I come from money! Why would I date you for your money? You don't know me at all."

Julie knew she sounded like a bad soap opera, but she couldn't seem to rein herself in.

Zan opened his mouth to refute her question when a large group of the awards recipients entered the room in high spirits.

"Jules, I have to go right now. Can we please talk later?" Zan's eyes begged her to soften towards him.

"We both have a job to do right now, so let's get it done, Zan. Or should I say **Mr. DeKeurge**?" Julie turned away to grab her camera for the photo shoot.

Zan looked down at the floor and then glanced over towards Julie, who had turned away from him and was very busy getting her camera settings ready.

Burying a sigh, Zan walked up towards the small stage that had been set up at the front of the event and where Selina was greeting the others who had just joined them in the room.

The rest of the evening went as expected between Julie and Zan, professional and stilted.

Julie was proud of herself, that she was able to work the event. A year ago, she would have been a weeping mess. Now, she'd pulled herself together and kept putting one foot in front of the other.

Her displeasure with Zan helped with that. She didn't think she'd ever felt that much hostility towards any person before in her entire life.

Even Spencer or Charlotte.

After the presentation of the donation to the Turks and Caicos groups, Zan made the usual rounds that he did at these affairs, shaking hands and thanking people for their work.

As the major donor, he found himself, at last, seated at one of the front tables with several island dignitaries.

Throughout the evening, it was easy for Julie to ignore him, except when she went around and got individual table shots of everyone there.

Other than that, Julie continued to do her job and so did Zan. In fact, they both did their jobs so well, that only Selina knew something was amiss.

Towards the end of the evening, Selina got quietly with Julie and let her know that she'd gotten all the shots the Chamber needed, so she could cut out if she wanted to.

Julie gave Selina a quick hug and thanked her. It wasn't too much longer that Julie was handing her parking stub to one of the attendants.

Standing on the curb with her duffels on either side of her, Julie was holding it together long enough for her to get home.

Her car was pulled up in front of her and she grabbed her bags and placed them in the back seat. Then she handed the parking attendant a tip and climbed into the driver's seat.

Just as her door was shutting, she heard Zan call out her name.

She refused to acknowledge that she'd heard his call and took off out of the parking lot and headed for home.

The silent tears couldn't be stopped as they rolled down her face.

Julie worked hard to focus on her driving through her grief.

She made it home in one piece.

Except for her broken heart.

So, she allowed herself a 60-minute pity-party and then went to bed.

And dreamt...

Chapter Twenty-One

FIGHT AT THE OKAY CORRAL

"What do you mean there is an emergency board meeting?" Elliot did not like this news.

"I'm sorry, Mr. Harris, for the last-minute notification. I was just now instructed to contact all board members."

Ana's voice was professional and smooth in the face of Elliot's verbal aggression.

Elliot wanted to have something on Jaimee before having to meet again with the board.

Just last week his investigator, Ian, had informed him that he was refunding the money Elliot had paid him to look into Jaimee's history, trying to find dirt.

Ian had told Elliot that since he was unable to come up with anything, he didn't feel right keeping the money and had direct deposited it back into the account Elliot had paid him from.

And now Elliot hadn't had time to find another investigator to do the job.

Elliot's voice changed, "All right, Ana. Thank you for letting me know. I will be there this evening."

He was able this time to hang up the call without destroying the phone.

Ana disconnected the call and looked up at Jaimee with a nod. Jaimee nodded back.

"Thank you, Ana. Are the rest of the board going to be able to make it?"

"To a person, they said they would not miss this for the world."

"Well then, let's get set-up."

Jaimee turned to the man standing next to the door.

"Do you need anything else before the meeting?" Jaimee smiled at the handsome man.

"No, Jaimee. We're ready to go."

Ian smiled back at the two women.

Elliot arrived at the Foundation's office, parked his car in the underground parking and took the elevator to the executive floor.

The doors opened and he headed down the hall to the board's conference room.

He entered the room and was instantly struck by how subdued everyone was. In fact, no one looked at him at all. Usually, there was the perfunctory "Hello" or "Good Evening."

But not tonight. It must be pretty serious if the board is this somber.

Elliot grabbed his usual choice of chair, which was at the other end of the conference table, opposite where Jaimee now sat, making some notes on a legal pad.

She did not look up or acknowledge him in any way.

Elliot straightened his tie and sat back, waiting for the meeting to commence.

Jaimee looked up and addressed the board.

"Thank you for meeting at the last moment tonight. I appreciate you all being here."

Several of the board members murmured acknowledgements or nodded back at her.

"Just what is so important, Jaimee?" Elliot was able to load the simple question with so many shades of disapproval.

Jaimee wondered how she'd ever missed that part of him before now.

Jaimee watched Elliot as the rest of the board members turned to look at him, many with frowns on their faces.

What the ...? Elliot felt unsettled and he didn't like that feeling. It was as though he was not in charge.

Just then the door to the conference room opened and two police officers entered, followed by Ian.

Elliot was still trying to wrap his wits around the situation when the officers walked directly over to him and one of them asked him to stand up.

"Why!?" Elliot's look of disdain and off-handed refusal to follow the officer's instructions caused a couple of the other board members to start to stand up in outrage at Elliot's behavior.

Jaimee asked them to please sit down and allow the law officers to continue.

The two board members nodded towards Jaimee and sat back down in their chairs; however, the scowls did not leave their faces.

And all that anger was directly at Elliot.

Elliot watched as Ian walked over to Jaimee and handed her some papers.

Jaimee rapidly flipped through them and passed them to the board member closest to her.

He looked them over and passed them to the person sitting across from him and so it continued until the papers arrived at Elliot's end of the table, where they were tossed to land right in front of him.

He reached out and picked up the papers with feigned boredom and started to read.

As his eyes continued down the first page, his face seemed to lose all its color.

By the time he'd reached the end of the second page, he was leaning forward over the table, raking one shaking hand through his usually neat hair and his lips trembled.

This was certainly a different man than any of them were used to seeing.

Jaimee's calm voice cut through the tension in the room like a hot knife through butter.

"Elliot. Please don't make a scene you'll regret. Just go with them."

Elliot looked over at the woman he had hoped to beat in the corporate game. He had been certain his plan would secure him a position of power at the DeKeurge Foundation.

After all, she was only a woman.

It was almost as if Jaimee could read his mind.

"Oh, by the way. You're fired."

And with that Elliot was arrested, handcuffed, and escorted out of the building and into the back of the police vehicle.

And with that Elliot was arrested, handcuffed, and escorted out of the building and into the back of the police vehicle.

Back in Jaimee's office, Ana put a hand on the young CEO's shoulder.

"I'm so proud of you, Miss Jaimee. I wish your father had been able to be here to see tonight's events."

"I wish so too, Ana.

But on second thought, I'm glad mom dragged him away for a two-week cruise. This would have been hard on him, the dissidence in the Board."

"Yes, but now you've proven you can handle just about anything. So, those other couple of board members will not be speaking less of you behind your back any longer."

Jaimee sighed out a breath of relief and turned to Ian.

"Thank you for your help. We had no idea that he was wanted in two separate countries for corporate crimes. You have been invaluable to the Foundation."

Ian smiled into Jaimee's eyes, "It was all pleasure for me.

"As I told you before, he had hired me to investigate you. When he told me to make something up about you, I suddenly felt the need to find out about his own history. Amazing what one can find if they look carefully enough. He was actually quite clever in his dealings. Almost good enough to get away with it all."

Ana scoffed and called Elliot a rude name. She was going to elaborate when Jaimee burst out laughing.

"Ana, you are so right!"

All three of them laughed at that point.

Ian was intrigued with the woman.

205

Jaimee was more interesting in the flesh than he'd found her to be online. And he'd found in his investigation just how memorable she actually was.

He hoped to stick around a little longer to find out much more.

Chapter Twenty-Two

LIFE GOES ON

"Julie, talk to me." Selina's soft voice over the phone line almost brought tears to Julie's eyes – again.

Julie sighed. She couldn't believe how much saltwater she'd produced over the past couple of days.

She'd spent that time holed up in her condo, cropping and finalizing the pictures for the Chamber.

She thought she'd pulled it together pretty well after her pity-party, but then out of the blue, she'd tear up again. It was getting on her nerves.

Why couldn't she just let it go!

"Sorry about that, Selina."

And then she had a thought.

"Would you like to come over and retrieve the flash drive with all the shots for the Chamber?"

Selina smiled and relaxed. "Julie, I'd love to. How about if I pick us up some dinner on the way?"

Julie felt better already. "It's sound like a great plan. See you around seven?"

"Great! See you then."

Julie looked around her condo and noticed the clutter.

Jumping into action she started cleaning up. It was one thing to have tissue boxes all over the place if it was just her, but it was another thing with company coming.

"So, Zan, what are you going to do?"

Zan didn't want to answer.

And why should he! He hadn't done anything wrong – had he?

Monica wasn't having any more of his excuses.

After all the times he had helped dig her out of whichever emotional hole she had dig herself into, now it was her turn to return the favor.

And she was determined that Zan was going to fix this.

She'd seen how much Zan had lightened up when he was with Julie.

She'd glimpsed the old Zan she knew from childhood, someone who was mostly happy and helpful, not somber and sometimes curt.

"Zan..." She waited for him to meet her eyes, which he finally did.

"What did you think was going to happen?"

Zan just shrugged. Now he was acting like an 8-year-old who didn't want to admit to something he'd done.

Monica softened her tone even more and repeated herself, "What did you think was going to happen?"

Zan raked his hands through his hair.

Why wasn't there some sort of manual about how to handle women?

Wait! Didn't that word 'handle' meant he was being kind of sexist?

Oh, geez, this was difficult.

Could someone please just tell him what to do? He could follow instructions.

He just couldn't foretell what Julie's reaction was going to be. And besides, he'd been caught off guard.

He hated being caught off guard.

Especially when something was important to him.

And Julie was very important to him.

Zan realized that Monica was waiting for an answer from him.

"I don't know. I guess I didn't think it would be that big of a problem for her." Zan sounded lost.

"Zan, you are one of the most giving and generous men I've ever known. You are kind. You are industrious. You are wonderful at those events with all the people your family is helping."

Hearing Monica's soothing words, Zan started to feel a little better about himself.

"But you are as dumb as a box of rocks when it comes to women."

What?!?

Zan's expression waivered somewhere between indignation and total confusion, which made Monica smile.

"Hon. You must admit that you don't know what you're doing here. If you want my help, and I would love to help you, you've got to be open to learning about the female psyche. At least a little. Is Julie important to you?"

Monica already knew the answer, but she wanted to hear Zan say it out loud.

"Is that a trick question?" Zan knew that Monica understood how important Julie was to him.

Or did she?

Ugh. This was getting complicated and Zan hated complicated.

"No, not a trick question. Is Julie important to you?"

Monica persisted in the face of Zan's discomfort with their discussion.

Zan chuffed out a hard breath. "Of course, she is. You already know that."

Monica's voice softened again, "Yes, I do. And now I know for certain that you know for certain."

Her smile of empathy made Zan relax.

"Why was that so hard for me to say out loud?" Zan really didn't recognize this version of himself.

"Maybe because the situation's outcome means so much to your future?" Monica tilted her head to one side.

Zan slowly nodded in agreement. After a moment he sat up straighter and looked directly at Monica.

"Okay, Obi-Wan, enlighten me. I'm ready to learn."

The next hour's conversation went back and forth; Zan showing his confusion and Monica gently guiding him into understanding.

By the end, Zan felt like he'd found a secret weapon that most men would give anything to have.

Especially if it worked like Monica said it would work.

Hmmm. Who would have thought that asking questions and having open dialogue (including a LOT more conversation than Zan was comfortable with) could potentially make a relationship easier to navigate.

"So, Julie, what are you going to do?" Selina had just spent the last hour listening to Julie sort through her thoughts.

As far as Selina could tell, Julie knew she was overreacting, but was also still clinging to the viewpoint that she was right and Zan was wrong.

Julie shrugged. "I guess I'm going to act like a grown-up?"

Selina smiled at her friend's obvious discomfort.

"I was really rude to Zan, wasn't I?" Julie sighed.

"I wouldn't say necessarily rude, but maybe a teeny bit hysterical." Selina smiled to soften her words.

The return smile from Julie was evidence enough that this conversation was going to turn out all right.

"So, what do I do to make this right? Maybe I've already blown any chance of a future with Zan."

Julie was disappointed with herself for her initial reaction in finding out that Zan had money.

Okay, so he has money. So what? Her family has money, too. Maybe not as much as Zan's family, but they certainly weren't struggling.

That wasn't the issue.

It was the fact that he had kept it a secret. Or, had **seemed** to keep it a secret.

Julie actually couldn't recall if they had ever talked about finances.

If he hadn't kept it a secret, then why had he looked so guilty at the banquet?

It just didn't make any sense.

Julie was, once again, pleased with noticing how much she'd been changing.

If this had happened last year, she would have been an emotional mess, roller-coasting from one day to the next.

Plus, it would have gone on for at least a week.

Now, she was able to confront it – albeit with some help from her friend – but she was confronting it now. And she didn't have that sickly feeling in her stomach she used to get.

"How do I fix this?"

Now it was Selina's turn to shrug.

"I'm not sure. I'm afraid this is something that you're going to have to figure out on your own."

They sat in silence for a moment or two.

Then Julie stated with some conviction in her voice, "And I will. But not tonight. Let's clean up from dinner and head out somewhere. Are there any local bands playing anywhere tonight?"

Selina was happy to see a spark of her friend return. She'd come over to Julie's tonight to help her get through this, and mission accomplished!

The next couple of weeks went by slowly.

They were pretty routine, workwise, for both Julie and Zan.

She had several meetings with the chamber regarding a few more projects. They really liked her style and wanted to keep her working with them as long as they could afford it.

Zan had several fishing excursions booked, so he was busy at sea.

Neither one of them tried to call the other.

They were both taking the time to do a deep dive on where their individual lives were going.

Zan had gotten what he wanted. His younger sister, Jaimee, was now CEO for the family business.

And she was apparently doing very well, as the rest of the Board of Directors had warmed up to her ideas to expand their reach for helping.

Then why did he have a feeling of incompleteness?

Even looking at expanding his charter business didn't bring him the joy he thought it would.

He'd already picked out the second boat and had been interviewing captains for it.

He thought he would feel more excited about the expansion.

Now instead, his thoughts were filled with Julie.

How she looked on his boat with the wind in her hair and a smile on her pretty face.

Or how she felt in his arms; like she was made perfectly for him.

He knew he needed to do something, but he wasn't sure what.

Monica had told him to think about it. And he had.

But he just hadn't come up with anything useful.

Zan guessed he'd just continue with the way things were for now, until he could find an idea that would work.

And so his life continued for the next several weeks.

Julie was enjoying her new projects.

One of them had to do with taking some shots of the group that was saving the coral reef around the Provo island.

It was amazing what had already been done by this dedicated team of scientists and volunteers.

She was getting some great shots with her underwater camera that were just stunning!

Luckily, she hadn't told her mom and dad anything yet about Zan.

So, at least she didn't have to explain why they were no longer hanging out together.

Julie actually looked forward to her calls with her parents, now that her mom had backed off.

In fact, life should be feeling pretty good right now.

But there was something that just felt empty.

Julie didn't run from that thought like she would have before.

Now she faced it and didn't flinch.

Although she no longer felt like she needed a man to have a full life, she missed Zan.

Could she go on without him? Sure.

Would she have the life she wanted? Probably.

Did she want to? No.

Okay, so now what?

Nothing. Julie was going to do nothing about it right now.

She didn't feel any urgency like she would have before.

A yearning? You bet.

But she could live with that.

And so, her life continued on the island for the next several weeks.

Chapter Twenty-Three

ON A WHITE HORSE - SORT OF

"It's called a grand gesture, Zan. Most women love them, if done right."

Monica wasn't being much help at all.

Zan wanted her opinion on how to approach Julie after all this time.

In fact, he was getting to the point that he wasn't sure that Monica wasn't just jerking his chain with all her "helpful input."

He still couldn't wrap his wits around her advice that most women would like a simple single flower given to them every once in a while, instead of a huge expensive bouquet of roses on Valentine's Day.

The bigger more expensive bouquet should count for more; showed he cared more – right?

Wrong, according to Monica.

Then she'd explained that the simple flower, hand delivered by the guy with a sweet kiss and a short statement of "I sure love you" or "Thank you for being in my life" would count for SO much more than that rose bouquet delivered once a year like clockwork.

Zan was starting to realize that even though most of the guys he knew who were in a relationship felt satisfied with how things were, that women seemed to want a little romance every now and then.

And not only when the guy wanted sex.

"It's called courting, Zan. A lost art which needs to be brought back."

When Monica grimaced, Zan thought that her tone of voice had given away a little more than she wanted it to.

"Anything you want to tell me?" Zan would be happy to have this conversation turned back on Monica instead of focused on him.

"Not at the moment, but thanks for asking, Zan"

Well, that hadn't worked.

"Okay, Monica. What sort of grand gesture are we talking about here?"

Zan leaned back in the lounge chair on his deck and crossed his arms over his chest.

When he realized that he looked like he was protecting himself, he relaxed a little bit.

"You know. Riding in on the white horse type stuff." Monica waved her hand in a small circle to indicate "whatever."

"You want me to ride a white horse?"

Zan knew that she had to be just messing with him at this point.

"No!" Monica showed her exasperation at Zan's seeming unwillingness to work with her.

Now Zan was irritated at his friend.

"Well, then what do you mean? Speak plainly, in one or two syllable word sentences please. Because I am NOT following you."

Monica sat up on the edge of the lounge chair she had been stretched out on and reached out a hand to Zan's arm.

"You don't horseback ride, Zan. You're a captain of a boat. What would you be able to do that would get her attention and impress upon her that you were serious about making a statement?"

Zan thought about it for a moment.

"Something with a boat... Okay, let me work on that."

He stretched back out on his back, closed his eyes, and seemed to doze.

Monica stretched back out on her lounge and waited.

"Okay, if you would all stand over here in front of the seawall, I'll get the full group shot for your website."

Julie got everyone arranged by height so that all faces could be seen in the camera.

The day was perfect for this shoot.

The bright blue sky was dotted occasionally by a fluffy white cloud, moving slowly in the gentle wind.

This particular beach was some of the whitest sand Julie had seen anywhere on the island.

The setting was stunning with all the rich colors.

Out on the ocean, several boats were moving about, some sailing with the breezes and some motoring to their destinations.

Just as Julie was getting the last couple of shots, she became aware of music reaching the shore from somewhere.

It was pretty. A love song from some movie, but she couldn't remember which.

"Okay, everyone! Just look back here towards the camera. We're almost done!"

Julie's cheerful voice didn't seem to be reaching some of the subjects of the shoot.

Instead their eyes seemed to be glued to something behind her.

Julie called out again. "Hi, everyone! Just look over here for a moment and then we're done!"

She'd made her voice a little louder since maybe they just hadn't heard her first request.

A couple of the men in the group pointed and smiled at something out at sea, while several of the women covered their mouths or placed an open palm over their hearts.

What the heck!?

In slight annoyance, Julie turned around to look for what was disrupting her photo shoot.

And then she just stood there with her mouth open like she was about to say "oh."

Coming at a pretty fast clip towards the shore was a small dingy boat with a man standing in it, guiding it with one hand on the tiller and the other holding up a bouquet of bright flowers.

Beyond the dingy was a boat.

And not just any boat.

It was Zan's boat and Robert and Pierre were standing on the lower deck, holding up a speaker where the music was coming from.

Julie's breath caught in her throat.

Zan.

His smile got larger as he got closer to the shore. He shut off the motor and the boat started gliding up onto the sand.

However, it was moving a little faster than he'd planned.

When the bow got about three feet up the shore, the rest of the dingy stopped dead in the water and Zan flew out of the boat and landed flat-out, face down in the sand, the bouquet buried underneath him.

Julie's eyes flew open with worry and she started heading towards him.

She got there at the same time he rolled over onto his back and spit out a mouthful of sand. The broken stems of the bouquet flowers looked like they had wilted.

He sat up and turned around to face his reason for doing this stunt.

Just then, Robert's voice carried across the water to the shore.

"Way to go, Uncle Zan!"

Julie finally reached Zan with a smile starting on her face. "Are you okay?"

"I think so. Just a little wounded pride."

Zan got to his feet and stood there covered in sand, holding the destroyed bouquet in front of him.

He just stared at Julie.

When had she gotten more beautiful?

She also held herself differently. More relaxed. Less stressed.

Basically, more sure of herself.

It looked great on her!

Julie thought Zan looked wonderful.

Although she knew his pride was hurt and he might be a little humiliated with the unintended prat fall, he kept his warm gaze on her.

Zan held out the flowers towards her.

The group that had gathered around them was waiting and watching with smiles on their faces.

This was better than watching any reality TV show!

Julie smiled at Zan and reached out and accepted the flowers.

To her, they were beautiful.

The stems of the yellow daisies were all broken, and the bouquet could have been described as sad, but to Julie they meant the world.

Zan brushed more sand off his face and out of his hair.

He stepped closer in front of her and took one of her hands in his.

"I've missed you so much, Jules. Please forgive me for being so dense."

Julie's heart melted.

"Actually, Zan, please forgive me for overreacting. I've come to understand how our quarrel came about."

"There's nothing to forgive."

Julie couldn't take her eyes off Zan's.

The emotion that was welling up in her was almost overwhelming.

Zan's heart was beating so fast, he was sure everyone could hear it.

He reached into his pocket and ... felt nothing. What?!

Zan let go of Julie's hand and raced back over to where he'd landed in the sand, digging around looking for something.

Two of the men in the group caught on and joined Zan in his quest.

"Aha!" One of the men held something out to Zan. All three men got back up and brushed sand off their pants.

Zan then went back over to in front of Julie.

And dropped to one knee.

Julie thought her heart was going to burst from her chest when she realized what Zan was doing.

And then the tears started.

Zan saw Julie start to cry and thought maybe he'd made a mistake.

When Julie saw the confusion cover Zan's face, she gave him a small smile and nodded for him to continue.

All the women sighed.

"Julie." Zan cleared his throat when his voice cracked.

He started again. "Julie.

"You are what I've been looking for my whole life. When I'm with you I feel stronger and more certain about my ability to conquer life. I hope you feel the same way about me."

Julie's smile got brighter, even through the tears streaming down her face.

"I love you, Julie, and I want to live with you for the rest of my life."

Zan smiled and waited for Julie to respond.

"And?" Julie thought Zan's look of bewilderment that turned into understanding was perfect.

"And, will you marry me?" Zan's words came out in a rush.

Julie kneeled down in front of Zan and placed the bouquet on the ground next to her.

Then she took his face in her hands.

"Yes, I will marry you, Zan."

He started to kiss her when he felt her hand on his chest.

Zan pulled back in confusion, looking at Julie, trying to figure out what he'd done wrong.

"Is there a ring, maybe?" Julie looked a little bit chagrined at asking the question.

"Oh! Yes!" Zan held up his other hand and opened the small velvet box.

All the women sighed again.

He placed the ring on Julie's finger, and everyone cheered; the crowd on the beach as well as Robert and Pierre on the boat.

The kiss was sweet – a little sandy, but sweet, nonetheless.

Chapter Twenty-Four

MEETING THE IN-LAWS

"Julie! That's wonderful!" Julie's mom couldn't contain her delight in hearing about her daughter's engagement.

Well, actually, she was more delighted now than she was 5 minutes ago in the conversation.

Now that she knew more about Zan – Alexander Roland DeKeurge of THE DeKeurge Foundation – things looked much brighter.

The fact that his family was what her family would call "new money" didn't lessen her happiness for her daughter.

Julie smiled to herself at her mom's newly found exuberance.

Boy, the tone of their conversation had changed fast after giving her mom the 411 on Zan's family background.

Of course.

"So, Hon. When are you coming home for a visit?" Julie's dad chimed in from the extension in the library of their Connecticut house.

"We thought we might fly up for the next weekend. Does that work with your schedule?"

Julie wanted Zan to meet her folks.

This was mostly to put her parents' minds at ease.

However, once Julie's mom found out about Zan's family, that part of it seemed to be a moot point.

"Next weekend sounds perfect! Do you need us to pick you up at the airport?"

Julie again smiled when she realized what her mom's reaction was about to be.

"We'll be landing at the Tweed New Haven Airport."

"Tweed? What airline are you using?"

"It's a private jet, Mom."

Silence.

Julie couldn't contain herself any longer and laughed out loud.

"We'll be flying in on Zan's family's plane."

Julie's mom stuttered for just a moment until she found her bearings.

"How nice! We so look forward to seeing you."

Julie knew her dad was rolling his eyes at her mom's Connecticut steel backbone coming through the phone line.

"I'll email you guys the details. We are SO looking forward to seeing you next Saturday! I love you."

As Julie ended the call, she enjoyed the fact that she hadn't felt any need to rub Zan's family's wealth in her mom's face – much.

And now to get ready to meet Zan's parents for dinner tonight!

Julie had spent quite an amount of time figuring what she should wear.

Zan hadn't been much help; he said to just wear something comfortable.

Comfortable as in only 2-inch heels instead of 4-inch?

Linen instead of silk?

Julie had been at her wits end until Selina called to see how she was doing.

"So? Meeting the parents tonight, eh?" Selina was so happy for her friend.

For a while there, it had been touch-and-go.

"Yes, and I don't know what to wear." Julie let out a sigh. "I really want to make a good impression with them."

"You could wear a potato sack and you'd still make a good impression, but I do understand.

"What about that peach-colored floor length cotton sheath dress I saw in your closet?"

"It's sort of casual. Do you think it would work?"

"Well, it is comfortable, isn't it?" Selina laughed.

"Absolutely! Come to think of it, I think you might be right. It's pretty, yet comfortable. If I pair it with my gold braided hoop earrings and a bangle bracelet, it might even pass for slightly upscale, just in case Zan's parents dress for dinner."

"You know, you could just call Ana at their office. She runs everything and would know what to wear for tonight.'

"I'm NOT going to bother the CEO's Administrative Assistant about what to wear tonight."

Julie paused for a moment. "I'll save that for bigger questions I will probably have later."

Selina laughed again.

"Call me tomorrow and let me know how it goes!"

"Thank you, Selina. I will. Bye."

"Bye."

Julie now had to figure out if she should wear her hair up or down.

Decisions, decisions!

Julie was nervous and she couldn't believe how unsettled she felt!

All because she wasn't sure if she was dressed correctly for meeting Zan's parents.

She took a deep breath and stepped out of Zan's car after he'd parked, turned off the motor, and come around to open her door.

"You look beautiful, Jules."

She took his outstretched hand and exited the vehicle.

Standing next to him felt very calming.

He leaned down and gave her a soft kiss before turning around and leading her to the front door.

Which was at the top of a long flight of stairs.

The steps were about 10 feet across from banister to banister and at least a foot deep.

By the time they reached the top, the front door was open and Zan's parents were standing there.

Completely dressed for an elegant dinner.

Mr. DeKeurge had on a dark blue suit and silk tie.

Mrs. DeKeurge was wearing a deceptively simply dinner gown which Julie knew cost a fortune.

Zan's mother had accompanied her dress with high heels and a triple strand of pearls with matching earrings.

Julie's heart dropped. She had SO underdressed.

She and Zan made it to the top of the steps.

"Mom and Dad, this is Julie. Julie, my mom and dad."

Zan was beaming from ear to ear.

Mr. DeKeurge reached out and gave Julie a hug.

"Welcome to the family, my dear!"

His voice was full of happiness.

Julie then turned towards Zan's mother and waited.

Finally, after what seemed like forever, Mrs. DeKeurge reached out and swept Julie into a huge hug.

"Thank goodness, I can go change out of this completely uncomfortable outfit! I was so worried when Zan told us we were meeting one of the United States founding families and I figured I needed to dress up!"

Julie leaned back from the hug and her mouth opened in shock for a moment and then snapped shut.

A giggle worked its way up and out of Julie's mouth and she and Zan's mom shared a moment of total understanding and laughter.

"Does that mean I can change, too?" Mr. DeKeurge was already loosening his tie while heading back into the house.

Zan just took in all of the happenings with a look of blank confusion on his face.

"Oh, Zan! Why didn't you tell us that tonight we could be ourselves! You made it sound like if we didn't make a good impression with Julie, you might lose her."

Zan's mother shook her head at her son as though he was addled.

She took Julie's hand and lead her into the house.

"Dear, you have a seat wherever you want and give me just a few minutes to put on my usual at-home ensemble. Zan, get Julie something to drink!"

And with that, Mrs. DeKeurge waved over her shoulder at the younger couple and joined her husband who was already moving upstairs to change into something else.

Julie turned towards Zan.

"Zan? What did you tell your parents about me?"

Zan was still standing there, trying to make sense out of what had just occurred.

When he'd first spotted his folks in the doorway, he couldn't figure out why they were wearing such formal outfits.

It looked as though they were waiting for the Queen to visit.

"Zan?"

Julie's voice finally penetrated Zan's mental fog.

"Huh?" Zan turned towards where Julie had finally settled on one of the sofas in the front room.

"What did you tell your parents about me?"

"Well, not much really. I just explained that your family had been one of the founding families in Connecticut. Wasn't that right?"

"Yes, but it makes us sound like snobs!"

"I never said that!"

"You didn't have to. You just left out the part that I'm pretty down to earth."

Zan rubbed the back of his neck in chagrin.

"I just did it again, didn't I? I think I need to put a little more thought into how I describe things."

Julie got back up and walked over to him, sliding her arms up around his neck.

"I imagine this is one of those traits that right now I find endearing, but in a few years, it will irritate me to no end."

Zan slipped his arms around Julie's waist.

"But you'll still love me – right?" Zan leaned down for a kiss.

Julie allowed herself to be swept into the kiss as it deepened.

Zan moved one gentle hand to the back of Julie's head and drank from her mouth.

Julie tightened her hold on Zan and moved into him leaving not one inch of space between them. Being in his arms was magical.

"Ahem." The quiet sound worked on Julie like a bucket of ice water had been dumped on her.

Zan took a little longer to come out of the wonderful haze he was in.

When Zan didn't let go of Julie, she put her hands on his chest and pushed him.

"What's wrong, Jules?" Zan looked down at her red face.

Julie shot her eyes to the side as she gave a slight nod in the same direction.

Zan eyes widened when he finally understood that his dad was standing there in the doorway to the front room.

"Sorry to interrupt what appears to be a very nice moment, but your mom's going to be here in less than a minute."

Mr. DeKeurge's face was averted towards another section of the room while he made the statement.

"Thanks, Dad." Zan grinned at his father's quiet humor as well as the red hue that had suffused Julie's face.

"It's okay, Jules. Mom and Dad know about sex. How do you think I got here?"

With what sounded like a muffled guffaw, Mr. D turned and headed into the dining room.

"Zan!" This evening was rapidly becoming nothing like she had envisioned.

And although she was a little embarrassed, she was starting to feel at home with the obvious warmth in Zan's family.

"Well! That feels better!" Mrs. DeKeurge came down the stairs in slacks, a brightly colored blouse, flat shoes, and a smile.

Gone were the pearls. She looked comfortable and happy.

"Julie, you must think we're nuts!" She swept over to Julie and took hold of her hands.

"Please let me start this again. Welcome to the family! We are so happy that Zan has finally found someone to love."

Mrs. D's smile couldn't have been wider or more genuine.

Julie smiled back at her soon-to-be mother in law.

"And I'm just as happy as you are!"

Looking at the two of the most important women in his life, Zan felt something release in his chest.

He knew looking at his mom and Jules that something wonderful was just beginning.

He hoped that Julie's parents would accept him into their family as well.

Chapter Twenty-Five

DOES ONE BOW OR JUST SALUTE?

Zan loved watching the various expressions flit across Julie's face on their flight from Providenciales to Miami for a quick Customs and Immigration check then back up into the sky and onto Connecticut.

She acted as though she'd never been on a private jet.

Zan was astonished to find out that she hadn't.

"We don't need a private jet to get around the United States!" Julie laughed at Zan's expression.

They both realized just how different their upbringings had been.

Zan was born and raised on an island. Small planes and private jets were how his family got around the islands, as well as trips to New York for business.

When Julie asked what type of business they did in New York, Zan explained that the Foundation's current accountant as well as their business attorney worked out of NYC.

When the Foundation had expanded so much under Zan's father as the CEO, they realized that their local accountant was unequipped to handle the larger amount of number-crunching.

So, they brought the accountant into their Foundation as an in-house financial officer and outsourced the full accounting and taxes to a firm they'd been referred to in the city.

The same for their legal department.

Julie then explained that her family's accountant and attorney were with the same accounting and legal firms that had handled Julie's grandparents and great-grandparents' accounts.

This information opened an entirely new area of discussion for the couple.

With the expansion of Zan's charter boat services, he knew that he needed to make some choices.

He and Julie needed to decide how they would handle taxes and such.

Do they put both their businesses under one corporation or do they keep everything separated?

However, this was a discussion for another day.

Today, it was the final leg of "meet the future in-laws."

Zan really hoped it went well!

Upon landing at the smaller airport in New Haven, their plane taxied to a hangar away from the main terminal.

Parked next to the hangar was a sleek black stretch limo, similar to the one that had driven Julie to the airport for her non-honeymoon trip so many months ago.

It felt like a lifetime ago. So much had changed, and all for the better.

Julie looked at the limo with a raised eyebrow.

What were her parents thinking? Why a limo?

Their jet stopped moving and the engines shut down.

One of the pilots opened the door and lowered the drop-down steps.

Then he went down the three steps first so he could hold out a hand for Julie to take while descending the steps.

"Thank you." Julie's smiled at the pilot.

When Zan reached the tarmac, he shook the pilot's hand.

"Thank you, Robert. As usual a very smooth ride."

"We'll see you Sunday afternoon?" Robert and his co-pilot would be taking the next 24 hours off and exploring NYC that evening.

"Unless you hear otherwise, that's the plan." Zan gave a small smile indicating that there was the slight possibility of a change.

The other pilot had already retrieved their luggage from the aft baggage area and had their overnight cases ready for them.

Julie thanked the pilot for her case and headed over towards the limo.

As she got close, the driver got out and took her bag.

Julie smiled at him.

It was Dave! The guy who drove her to the airport before!

"Hi!" Julie was happy to see him.

"Hi!" Dave grinned as he put her bag into the trunk of the vehicle.

He came back and took Zan's luggage and placed it next to Julie's.

Then Dave opened the back door of the limo.

And there was Julie's mom and dad, dressed to the hilt.

What the heck?

Dave reached out a hand to help Julie's mom out of the car.

Immediately following Mrs. Anderson was Julie's dad, who swept Julie up in a big hug.

"Hon! It's so good to see you!"

Julie hugged her dad back and then turned to her mom and received a stilted conservative half-hug.

Julie frowned at her mom before turning towards Zan.

"Zan, these are my parents. Mom and Dad, this is Zan."

Mr. Anderson stepped forward with a smile and shook Zan's hand.

"We're so glad to meet you, Zan!"

Her dad's exuberance made up for her mom's lack of warmth.

Zan then turned to Julie's mom and waited to see what he was supposed to do – handshake or hug?

It surprised both Zan and Julie when her mom held out her hand, palm down, as though Zan was supposed to kiss it or something.

Julie's dad just rolled his eyes in amusement as he stepped forward and placed an arm around his wife's shoulders. "Margo, just relax."

Julie had never seen her mom act so weird before; and there had been plenty of weird opportunities in the past.

"Mom? What's up?"

Julie stepped in between her mom and Zan and faced her mom with a low voice.

"What are you doing?"

"I'm greeting my future son-in-law." Her mom didn't even smile.

In fact, she looked almost like she was in pain.

"Okay, but why are you acting like this. And **why** are you dressed like that?"

Julie indicated her mom's hat with a wave of her hand.

"I'm trying to make a good impression."

Margo's voice was so quiet that Julie could barely hear what she'd said.

"A good impression?"

Julie glanced at her dad who just stood there with an arm around her mom and almost laughing.

"Dad?"

Julie's dad leaned forward and in a very loud stage whisper stated, "We don't want to make a wrong move in front of the billionaire!"

At that, Julie threw up her hands and turned around to look at Zan.

He had started to laugh, when he realized the situation.

Julie's dad joined in the mirth and the two men shook hands again.

"Stop it!" Julie's mom hissed at her husband. And that sent the men into more mirth.

Finally, Margo looked at her daughter with an expression of disappointment.

"I so wanted to do this right. And now I've failed."

Julie couldn't help but smile at her mom's predicament.

She finally understood that her mom had wanted to impress Zan somehow.

Which, Julie considered, was a good sign.

If her mom wanted to impress her future husband, then that future husband would probably be able to handle her mom just right.

"Mom, relax."

Julie gave her mom another hug and then turned to Zan who reached out, took one of Margo's hands, and kissed the back of it.

"Believe me, Mrs. Anderson. You've made a great impression on me. The fact that you care so much about what I think of you makes me feel very welcome."

Julie's mom's face changed into one of astonishment.

"I don't care about what you think of me!"

Her eyebrows raised almost to the top of her forehead.

"I wanted to do the socially correct action and I wasn't sure what to do!"

Zan, Julie, and her dad just stood there looking at Margo with questions on their faces.

Dave quietly slipped back into the front seat of the limo and gently shut his door.

Julie's mom looked at them and then wrung her hands a little bit.

"I apologize. That came out wrong. I meant to say that I wasn't sure what the proper protocol was for this sort of first meeting. And I'm afraid I blew it. Julie, I'm sorry."

This was one of the most sincere apologies Julie had ever heard from her mom – to anyone!

"Mom. It's okay! Just be yourself. Well, your at-home self, not your society self."

Julie's mom turned to Zan and held out her hand to shake this time.

"Zan, I apologize."

Zan reached out and scooped Julie's mom into a big hug. He lifted her off the ground a little bit and made happy noises while he did it.

Margo started to laugh. "Put me down! You'll hurt your back."

Zan released his hold on her and shook his head. "Nope. You weigh hardly anything at all. My back is not in danger of damage."

And so, the awkward moment disappeared.

They all climbed into the back of the limo, without Dave's help, and Zan closed the door from the inside.

Dave rolled down the privacy window and asked, "Where would you like me to drive now?"

Julie's dad spoke up, "Is anyone hungry? We could stop by the country club on the way home for a bite."

"Let's just head home, Dad. You and mom need to get into regular clothes."

"Thank goodness!" Julie's dad's huge sigh of relief made everyone laugh.

"Let's head to my parent's house, Dave."

"Okay." And the window rolled back up.

The short drive home was very pleasant for everyone.

⚬

"Mom! You already booked the church!?"

Julie couldn't believe her mom did that. Or maybe, she realized, she should just stop being surprised.

She'd had a lifetime to learn how her mom worked.

"Yes, I did. You know how fast it gets booked for weddings and a Christmas wedding would be so lovely, don't you agree?"

Margo couldn't understand her daughter's displeasure.

Julie took a slow deep breath. "Mom. Zan and I are getting married on the island."

"But it's so hot and sandy and ... well, it's just not Connecticut."

"Mom." Julie put a hand on her mom's knee.

"I know you mean well. I truly do. But this is my wedding, not yours, and I'd like to have the wedding of my dreams. And now, my dreams include a wedding on a white sand beach, with bright colors and bare feet."

Margo could only shudder a little.

"Bare feet?"

Julie laughed.

"Mom, it's all the rage. Brides love the idea of a beach wedding. In fact, it's possible that this could become Connecticut's destination wedding of the season!"

Julie figured it wouldn't hurt to put that out there.

She knew her mom wanted some column inches under the Wedding section in the newspaper.

Julie's mom paused to consider that.

"Would people actually fly there just for a wedding?"

"Mom! It's an Anderson wedding! Of course, they will. Especially if we ask certain members of society to mention that they intended to attend."

Julie continued, "Zan's family can book one of the pricey beach hotels for the weekend and pay for the flights."

She knew that Zan would be fine with that, since they had already discussed logistics.

As soon as Julie's mom started jotting down notes in her planner, Julie knew she'd won this particular battle and relaxed.

For the moment.

Next would come the dress.

Chapter Twenty-Six

MAHI-MAHI MATRIMONY

Julie stood in front of the full-length mirror and looked in awe and disbelief at the pretty girl in the wedding dress.

This girl looked happy and perfectly contented.

Her hair fell down past her shoulders in soft sun-highlighted waves.

The long, flowing white dress was perfect.

Her make-up consisted of a little eyeliner, mascara, and a soft peach lipstick. Foundation wasn't needed, since Julie's skin glowed from within with health and sunshine.

What a difference the past eighteen months had made.

Not just physically, but mentally as well.

Julie had become herself; not someone that others thought she ought to be, but the woman she knew she could be.

She felt centered and stable with her life.

Even though she was more even-keeled, she felt emotions more deeply.

With that thought, she gently placed a hand over her abdomen and a warm glow spread throughout her.

She had a wedding surprise for Zan.

She didn't show yet, at only 9 weeks along, but she was glad her wedding dress was not closely fitted.

For today, this secret was hers alone and tonight she'd tell her new husband.

He was going to be ecstatic.

Zan had stated he wanted to start their family right away.

Well, this was as close to right away as Julie could get.

The door to the bridal suite opened and her friends came in, smiling and laughing with happiness.

"Julie! You look wonderful!"

Selina – Julie's Maid of Honor – was breathtaking in her own right. Her flowing aquamarine dress made her beautiful eyes stand out.

She was holding Julie's bouquet in one hand and her own in the other.

Right behind Selina was Julie's friend Cate and then Zan's little sister, Jaimee. Both were wearing similar dresses, but in different shades of blue.

Their bouquets contained the same flowers as Julie's; local island varieties in cream, pink, and soft greens.

Julie's bouquet included a few strands of orchids hanging down from the bottom of it.

These same flowers also decorated the aisle and the canopy that was set up for the ceremony.

Julie's mom had finally embraced the style of wedding that Julie and Zan wanted.

When she had observed the decorating of the venue on the beach that morning with the softly flowing pink silk scarves attached to the backs of the white rattan chairs and all the flowers everywhere, she told Julie that it was exactly perfect.

The fact that the pictures for the paper back in Connecticut would be original and eye-catching only secured her approval even more.

Julie smiled at her mom as she came into the bridal suite right behind her bridesmaids.

Her mom was in her version of island-casual; a silk taupe and cream-colored calf length dress.

The sprinkling of sea green Swarovski crystals around the bottom of the dress matched the ones on the Bride's and bridesmaids' dresses.

The crystals would help keep their hems from flying up if a breeze came along. Not only beautiful, but practical as well.

Behind Julie's mom was the woman she now considered her second mother.

Zan's mom had secured one of the island's exclusive retreats for the wedding weekend.

This was their wedding gift for the couple.

The bridal suite was in a building set off from the other teakwood condos, which all had private beach or pool entrances.

Each of the 16 condo buildings had two separate living quarters, so everyone had some privacy for the weekend.

The main building at the entrance housed the restaurant and was where the reception would be held after the ceremony.

"Oh, you look lovely, Julie!" Zan's mom was smiling at the young woman who had captured her son's heart.

"Thank you, Momma." Julie's mom was "Mother" or "Mom," but Zan's mom was "Momma."

It had happened that first evening when Julie met Zan's family. The two women were in the kitchen after dinner, cleaning up when Julie had called her "Mrs. DeKeurge."

She'd turned to Julie and asked, "Would you be willing to call me Momma? It's what my mother called her own mother-in-law and I always thought it was the perfect title. I would love to be called that by you."

Julie's eyes had filled with happy tears as she hugged the woman who was now her Momma. She wasn't replacing her mother, but instead had doubled her family.

Following Zan's mom into the room was the wedding photographer.

She was a friend that Julie had met several years ago when she'd attended the Brooks Institute in Santa Barbara, California to learn photography.

"All right, Ladies! Time for some getting-ready shots."

The photographer was professional, friendly, and exuded calm – a trait that consistently earned 5-star reviews from her clients.

The next 30 minutes were fun and relaxing.

❧

Zan couldn't figure out where his nervousness was coming from.

He'd been just fine, right up until a minute ago when the minister had joined him in the living room of his temporary quarters for that weekend.

After the wedding and reception, he and his bride would retire to the suite that was currently housing the bride and her entourage with all the women involved with the wedding.

Well except for his Best Man – Best Woman – whatever. Monica.

Zan knew it wasn't usual to have a female as the Best Man, but if it hadn't been for his lifelong friend, he wouldn't be marrying the woman of his dreams today.

So, after a long conversation with Julie and his folks, he'd finally been convinced to give Monica the honor of standing up with him at the wedding.

It also helped that Julie and Monica were now best buds.

But sometimes, he didn't like it when they ganged up on him. They did it with love, but it still stung a little.

"Are you ready, Son?" Zan's father, who had been there for the past hour, asked the question after the minister had declared it was time.

Zan took a deep breath to calm his accelerated heartbeat.

Both his dad and the minister laughed when Monica slapped him on the back.

"Of course he's ready. He's been ready for ages."

Monica's smile lit up her face, watching her friend battle with his nerves. "It's just the usual pre-wedding jitters that most men get. It must be something in the male DNA that makes every groom a little bit nervous."

The minister and Zan's dad exchanged nods of agreement with Monica's statement.

Zan just shot a side look at his "Best Man."

Monica's outfit was similar to his own, cream-colored lightweight shirt and loose-fitting slacks.

Zan's was the same shade as his bride's dress (according to what he'd been told since he hadn't been allowed to see the dress before the wedding) and Monica's was a slightly darker hue.

"Let's do it!" Zan slipped on his flip-flops and headed for the door.

One of the fun – and interesting – parts of today was the Bride's and Groom's choice of gifts to everyone at the wedding; custom made flip-flips for everyone to wear on the beach for the ceremony itself. They had also scheduled pedicures at the retreat's spa for anyone who asked.

After the ceremony, everyone was welcome to clean off their feet and slip on shoes for the indoor reception, but their family and friends all agreed it would be fun to have everyone in matching footwear on the beach.

The only almost-holdout was Julie's mom. "One does not wear flip-flops at a wedding."

However, she'd changed her mind the night before when Julie took her down to the beach where the ceremony was being held.

Margo's shoes had immediately filled with sand and felt so uncomfortable that she had to remove them and walk barefoot.

Which in and of itself was fine until she stepped on a small shell. Now she understood the reason for the beach footwear.

Luckily, Julie had ordered a pair of flipflops for her mom that were as swanky as flipflops could get.

Now it was time for the ceremony to begin.

The small group of guests had found seats on the white wicker chairs set up so there was an aisle for the wedding party to walk down.

A three-piece music combo was playing softly in the background.

Then, the minister walked down to the canopy with Zan and Monica, who stopped to greet friends and family along the way.

Next, Zan's dad escorted his mom up the aisle to a couple of open seats at the front, also greeting friends and family.

Right behind Zan's parents came Julie's mom, escorted by one of Zan's friends. She looked relaxed and happy.

In fact, Julie's mom was beaming.

As they got to the front of the aisle, she stopped and posed for the photographer who had already been instructed on what was the best angle for pictures of her.

After she sat down and her escort grabbed a seat on the other side of the aisle, the music changed to a more somber tune.

Although the Caribbean lilt of the performance kept it upbeat, it was a bridal procession.

First, coming down the aisle was Cate, looking stunning.

As she got towards the front, she waved a small wave to her sister, Kristy who was sitting next to her husband Jackson.

Kristy was very pregnant with their first but had been able to get her doctor's approval for the private jet flight to the wedding.

The fact that Jackson wouldn't let her do anything except eat and rest made the long trip much easier.

Sitting on the other side of Kristy was Cate's weekend date. He winked at Cate and brought a blush to her cheeks.

Cate took her place at the far left of the canopy.

Next, Zan's sister Jaimee came up the aisle.

Zan hadn't realized how much his little sister had grown into her position as CEO of the Foundation until recently.

She'd actually gotten the Board holdouts to agree to her ideas of expansion.

It had taken tact and perseverance, but she'd accomplished the impossible.

And now it even looked as though she'd found the right guy.

Jaimee smiled at Ian who was sitting close to the aisle. His open smile back at her made her feel wonderful.

As Jaimee took her place next to Cate, Selina started up towards the flower-draped canopy.

She wore a look of contented joy on her face as she glided up to where the others were standing.

After Selina took her place and turned towards the back, the music again changed, and everyone stood up.

Julie, on her father's arm, started up the aisle. She was glowing with happiness.

Zan was mesmerized by her.

Their eyes met and didn't leave each other until she turned to give her dad a kiss on the cheek before he turned and sat down next to her mom.

Everyone else followed his lead and also sat back down, leaving just the minister and the wedding party, standing under the beautiful canopy.

The short ceremony was casual yet sincere. The minister stated the vows and both Zan and Julie repeated them, pledging their lives to each other.

Julie only choked up once, but after a deep breath was able to continue when Zan's hands gave hers a slight warm squeeze.

His eyes held all the love in his heart he felt for this wonderful woman.

When he slipped the ring on Julie's finger, his hands trembled slightly with the emotion that was welling up inside of him.

However, when the minister finally announced he could kiss the bride, he didn't hold back.

Zan completely stole Julie's breath away with the heated kiss he gave her.

Their family and friends hooted and applauded when he bent her slightly back as the kiss deepened even further.

Finally, the minister jokingly looked at his watch and tapped Zan on the shoulder.

When they came up for air, Zan was grinning with joy and Julie wore a happy, slightly flustered smile on her face.

Wow. That had been some kiss!

She turned and Selina handed back her bridal bouquet with a warm hug. Then Zan pulled Julie's other hand through his arm and they headed back up the aisle to the bright Calypso music that accompanied them.

Everyone was on their feet, smiling and cheering them. Hugs, kisses, and back slaps occurred and what had been an organized seating arrangement became a happy crowd that moved towards the reception venue.

Once everyone was inside the building, enjoying drinks and hors d'oeuvres, the photographer grabbed the Bride and Groom and the wedding party to head back to the beach for a few more photos. Less than 15 minutes later they were all back at the reception.

Some of the guests had gone back to their condos to put on regular shoes while others remained in their flipflops.

Both Zan and Julie changed into comfortable shoes for the reception.

Surprisingly, Julie's mom didn't. She seemed to be very much enjoying her foot-freedom.

The reception went the way of most receptions.

Good food and lots of drinks.

Several toasts were given to the newly married couple; some sweet, some rowdy.

Cake cutting – and no mashing cake in the face.

Zan had been warned by Monica that if he wanted a happy life, he needed to treat Julie like she was precious to him.

Which she was.

Bouquet toss, which Jaimee won to her mom's delight.

And lots of dancing to the DJ's wonderfully wide assortment of genres.

When it finally came time for the wedding couple to head over to their bridal suite, they were showered with birdseed, which would be gone before morning, making the local birds very happy.

Their suite had been handled by the venue help during the wedding and reception so that Zan's items had all been moved over to join Julie's.

There were more flower arrangements placed throughout the suite, and a fully stocked kitchenette promised they wouldn't have to be disturbed by ordering room service.

When they got to the entrance to the suite, Zan opened the door and lifted Julie in his arms.

He carried her into the suite, closing the door behind him with one foot.

Then he rapidly set down his bride and barked "Ow!" while grabbing his bare foot and hopping over to one of the soft chairs in the suite.

"Oh, Babe! What happened?" Julie's face showed her concern as she knelt down next to his chair, where he was massaging his injured foot.

"When I shut the door, I banged the side of my foot on it. I didn't know the foot had a funny bone!"

Zan grimaced as he rubbed away the pain.

"Well, I certainly hope this doesn't put a damper on our wedding night!"

Julie's eyes lit with humor when she realized that Zan's injury was more startling than severe.

Zan immediately let go of his foot and pulled Julie up onto his lap.

"Baby. Never." He cupped Julie's face in one of his hands and lowered his mouth to hers.

This kiss was gentle and complete.

Pulling back, he looked at Julie's face.

"There's something about you, Julie. I can't put my finger on it, but you're even more beautiful than usual. Is this what a wedding does to brides?"

Julie's smile was almost mysterious, like da Vinci's Mona Lisa.

"I suppose there might be a good reason for the change you see."

Zan tilted his head to one side in question.

Julie couldn't resist telling him any longer.

She took Zan's hand from her face and placed it over her abdomen, holding it there with hers.

Zan's puzzlement turned to wonder and then complete joy.

"Really? A baby? You're pregnant!?"

Zan couldn't contain his happiness and stood up with Julie in his arms and twirled around.

Laughing, Julie pleaded, "Zan! Stop spinning. Please!"

Zan immediately stopped and gently lowered Julie to her feet in front of him, placing one of his hands back on her abdomen.

His instant concern was charming and endearing.

"I'm not made of glass. I just can't do too much circular stuff like that. It unsettles my stomach a little bit."

"I noticed you didn't have any champagne at the reception today."

"I also haven't had any coffee since finding out I was pregnant. I really miss coffee."

Julie's wry smile made Zan smile, too.

"Jules, I'm going to take such good care of you – and our baby. When is it due?"

"Around Christmas."

Zan picked up Julie and hugged her again, this time more gently.

He pulled back his face and looked down into hers with concern.

"Can we still ... you know?"

Julie's laughter filled the room.

She put both her hands on the sides of Zan's face and pulled him to her for a heated sensual kiss.

At the end of the kiss, Zan just grinned and gently picked Julie back up. He turned around with his bride in his arms and headed for the bedroom.

Julie had just given him the best wedding gift ever.

A child.

Their child.

Now they were truly a family.

Epilogue

THREE YEARS LATER

Julie shaded her eyes to look out towards the ocean.

There was Zan standing in the water, waist high, holding their son in front of him.

"Mama! Watch! I swim! I swim!"

Zan gently lowered the youngster into the water and the child started to dog paddle, his head above the water.

From about a year old, Rogan had taken to water like a fish.

Zan had first wanted to teach him to float on his back, but Rogan had other ideas and had immediately flipped over and gone underwater, grinning and swimming.

Zan had picked his child up out of the water with alacrity, but relaxed when he realized that Rogan had held his breath.

From there on, he kept a close eye on the kid around any body of water, since you could bet that was where Rogan wanted to be.

Zan assumed that Rogan would become a proficient swimmer with age, but for now, he maintained a father's watchful eye.

When Zan picked Rogan back up out of the ocean, Julie waved at her son with enthusiasm.

"Good job, Rogan!"

Rogan threw his arms up like a boxing champ who had just won the round.

Julie and Zan both laughed with delight at their child's antics.

"Are you fellas hungry yet? I've got sandwiches made in the kitchen."

With that, both Zan and Rogan whooped and headed for shore.

Julie lumbered to her feet and was slowly heading towards their house when they caught up with her.

"How are you feeling?" Zan's hand went to the Julie's huge rounded front.

She was due any day, and every move felt cumbersome.

Zan thought she looked the epitome of womanhood, carrying his child.

And sexy as all get-out.

Julie thought she looked like a whale.

As they finished up their sandwiches, Julie stood to carry the empty plates to the sink and stopped.

She set the plates back down on the table and turned towards Zan with one hand on the small of her back and one hand over her abdomen.

"Zan. I think it's time."

"Time for what, Babe?"

Zan was helping Rogan wipe off his face with a damp washcloth laughing when Rogan tried to duck from the cloth with an impish grin on his face.

Julie rolled her eyes at Zan's nonchalance because she knew it would change to instant action when it hit him.

And that happened right about then.

"The baby!"

Zan jumped up and picked up Rogan in his arms, heading for the front door.

He arrived at the portal, stopped and turned around, noticing that Julie wasn't following.

Instead, she had started up the stairs.

"Where are you going?" Zan's voice pitched up an octave. Rogan's countenance got serious.

"I'm taking a shower and shaving my legs before we head to the hospital."

"What!?" Boy, you could take the girl out of Connecticut, but not Connecticut out of the girl.

"What if the baby comes now?"

Julie continued slowly up the stairs.

"We have plenty of time, Zan. The contractions are just starting."

Julie reached the top of the stairs and headed towards their bedroom suite.

She'd already packed her to-go bag and had picked out what she was wearing to the hospital.

Zan and Rogan appeared in the doorway of their bedroom as Julie headed to the bathroom.

"Mama? You okay?"

Julie turned around and smiled at their son. "Yes, Ro. I'm very okay. I think you might get to meet your little sister today!"

Zan sat Rogan on the floor when he wiggled to get down. The child ran over to his mother and wrapped his arms around her legs.

"I'm so happy!" As he looked up into her face, Julie's heart melted.

And then she grimaced and stood up straight.

Zan understood what was happening and picked his son back up.

"Hey, Sport! Let's go call your grandma and tell her the news!"

Zan and Julie silently agreed over Rogan's head.

The plan was that Zan's parents would come over to the house and stay with Rogan for a few days until Julie came home from the hospital.

Julie finished her shower and was dressed and heading down the stairs with her go-bag when Zan's parents arrived.

"Good luck, Julie!" Zan's mom gave Julie a gentle hug. "We'll take good care of your little guy."

"I know you will. Thank you so much for doing this." Julie hugged her back.

Then she turned and gave Rogan a hug.

"See you tomorrow or the next day, Ro. And, you'll be the big brother!"

"Bye, Mama!" Rogan was already engrossed in the game his grandpa was setting up for him in the family room and headed there as soon as Julie let go.

"Time to go, Jules." Zan gently took the bag from Julie's hand and guided her out the front door towards the waiting car.

"What a healthy little girl!" The labor midwife smiled at the couple, who were obviously in love with each other as well as their new baby.

The labor had been fast and intense, and Julie had handled it like a pro.

Zan, on the other hand, had needed to sit down after Livia was born, he was so overcome with emotion.

His strong wife had come through labor and given him the most perfect baby girl.

And here he was weak-kneed with tears running down his face.

One of the midwives handed him a bottle of water and a couple of tissues.

Julie could only smile at the love emanating from Zan as she wiped away her own tears of joy and cradled her new child in her arms.

She'd finally found her place in life.

She'd found her happiness.

She had found herself.

THE END

Join Pat's Mailing List

Sign up for my newsletter at www.patadeff.com to learn about new releases!

Also By Pat Adeff

THE SECOND CHANCES DO HAPPEN SERIES

Book 1: Take Another Chance
Book 2: Mahi-Mahi Matrimony
Book 3: The Romance Writer and the Geek
Book 4: To Heal A Heart
Book 5: In His Arms

Can You Help?

I love hearing from my readers!

If you liked this book, please leave a review on Amazon or Goodreads!

If you didn't like something about this book, please email me at pat@patadeff.com and tell me about it. I want to give my readers the best possible reading experience!

About The Author

Author Quote: "I value my life by how many people I help."

Pat Adeff writes sweet romances about second chances - with just a hint of spice!

She's also written several laugh-out-loud comedies which have been produced in theaters from California to New York.

She loves writing, reading, and cooking. If you sign up for her newsletters, you'll probably find a few of her favorite recipes attached.

Pat is an incurable romantic and definitely believes in second chances and happily-ever-after's. In fact, several years ago she found her own second chance! She and her composer husband recently moved from NYC to Largo, FL and are enjoying the sunshine!

Made in the USA
Las Vegas, NV
17 July 2023

74832986R00163